PRISONERS

Simon Tyree—He was the Navaho Stage Line's best driver, and he would deliver his passengers and the big railroad payroll unharmed and in one piece—or die hard trying.

Billy Starbuck—Beneath the arrogant talk and flashy dress of the Territory's most celebrated shootist lay a confused boy trying to prove himself a man.

Elizabeth Simpson—Beautiful, spoiled and selfish, her charms made her irresistible and her greed made her dangerous.

Kyle Lassiter—Until Billy Starbuck's first robbery cost him an arm, he was a top railroad security guard. Now he lived only for the day he could take his revenge.

Rebecca Simpson—A courageous frontier woman, years of marriage to a harsh, uncompromising man had not broken her spirit, but she had never known love until she met Simon Tyree.

The Stagecoach Series
Ask your bookseller for the books you have missed

STAGECOACH STATION 22:

DEVIL'S CANYON

Hank Mitchum

 Created by the producers of
Wagons West, White Indian,
and **Saga of the Southwest.**

Chairman of the Board: Lyle Kenyon Engel

BANTAM BOOKS
TORONTO • NEW YORK • LONDON • SYDNEY • AUCKLAND

STAGECOACH STATION 22: DEVIL'S CANYON

*A Bantam Book / published by arrangement with
Book Creations, Inc.*

Bantam edition/February 1986

*Produced by Book Creations, Inc.
Chairman of the Board: Lyle Kenyon Engel*

ISBN 0-553-25421-9

Published simultaneously in the United States and Canada

PRINTED IN THE UNITED STATES OF AMERICA

O   0 9 8 7 6 5 4 3 2 1

STAGECOACH STATION 22:

DEVIL'S CANYON

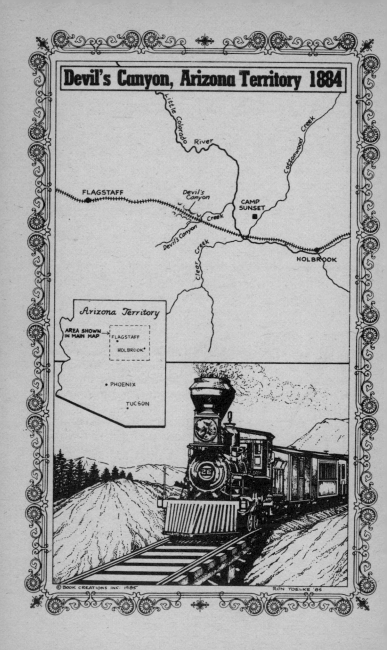

Chapter One

September had painted the high country between Holbrook and Flagstaff with its most brilliant colors. Vibrant splashes of red and yellow stood out against the dark green of the tall Ponderosa pine, and the valleys of Arizona Territory lay rich and deep in the amber hues of ripe, wild grain.

The sound of laughter intruded on the natural quiet as a mounted figure appeared on the distant horizon. He moved across the valley, his mule belly-deep in the wild grass, the sleek-coated beast playing an impromptu game of tag with a startled jackrabbit.

The young man was clad in the simple homespun bib overalls, chambray shirt, and round-toed, flat-heeled boots of the valley farmers, with a broad-brimmed, dome-crowned straw hat on his head and a small-bore rifle carried easily in his right hand. Yet there seemed no real purpose to his wanderings.

Then the man pulled his mount to a halt. He slid from the animal's sweat-stained, bare back and stood in the gravel roadbed of the newly laid railroad. The rifle rested comfortably in the crook of his arm as he stared off into the mountains that rose in quiet dignity in either direction.

To the east, beyond the wide trestle that spanned Clear Creek, lay Holbrook. In the opposite direction,

some distance beyond Cañon Diablo—Devil's Canyon—
lay Flagstaff.

The young man spoke as if he were not alone—as if
the mule were listening and could understand. He was
small and compact, and his blue eyes burned and danced
with the mystic fire of a born dreamer. "Here," he said,
marking the place in the gravel with the heel of his boot
and gouging out a shallow furrow.

The mule snorted and lowered his head to sniff at the
spot. A look akin to impatient disdain touched the animal's
dark brown eyes as he lifted his head. Eager to go home,
to go back to the barn, he pawed the ground.

Eighteen-year-old Will Simpson ignored the animal's
silent censure. Old dreams filled his head, as real to him
as the stories he had read in the dog-eared dime novel
that was stuffed in his back pocket. There were riches out
there beyond the mountains, riches of the kind not stored
in Heaven. *Gold. Greenback dollars.* Tangible wealth
a man could spend on earth—not like the so-called spirit-
ual rewards his older brother was always preaching about.
"Here," he said again, more determined than before.
Right here. His mind made up, the young man dug into
the bib above his waist and took out the dynamite he had
stolen from the shed behind his brother's barn.

Quickly, Will bent down and placed two sticks of the
explosive in the furrow he had dug with his boot—under a
length of the gleaming iron rail, just at the place where
the twelve-foot piece of steel was joined to another. He
stood up, viewing his handiwork. The two sticks looked
small and insignificant beside the heavy steel, like nothing
more than a pair of penny firecrackers. Will shook his
head and dug into his shirt a second time. And then,
judiciously, he bent down to add four more sticks of
dynamite to the first two. He tamped them into place with
the toe of his boot.

Smiling, the would-be train wrecker laid out the long
fuse. He trailed it down and across the yellow rock, leading the mule as he went, the long black string snaking
across the loose gravel as it wound into the tall grass and

disappeared behind a cluster of wind-worn boulders. Pulling the reluctant mule with him, Will clambered into the shelter of the rocks.

Will rested for a time and rolled himself a cigarette. He was a novice, pretending to be an expert. The tobacco wadded up in the center of the paper when he twisted the ends, but it didn't matter. With a flourish, he lit the smoke, inhaled, coughed, and then touched the cigarette's cherry tip to the end of the sulfur-caked fuse.

It seemed to take forever for the sputtering spark to crawl across the rocky terrain. Holding his ears, Will bobbed up and down three times from behind the rocks to watch. Finally, the charge detonated.

There was the mighty roar of man-made thunder, and then the smoke slowly cleared, the yellow haze lifting up through a constant rain of wood chips and pea-sized gravel. Twisted steel spiraled upward toward the blue sky, colored by the slow, dry rain of dust and debris.

A softer sound echoed and rumbled in the heads of the young man and the terrified mule, their hearing partially gone. And then there was silence, total silence. Together, they watched as a subtle change occurred on the face of the cliff directly across from them. Slowly, majestically, the black granite heaved outward, receded, and began to collapse.

The massive rock slide rumbled down from the uppermost reaches of the high mountain, growing in force as one mass of granite collided with another and another. The entire face of the landscape changed. Tall ponderosa pines on the lower slopes were uprooted and torn away as the mountain collapsed from within, the thundering of the huge black boulders pierced by the high-pitched whine of the splintering green wood as an entire grove of trees was torn apart and swallowed up by the hungry earth.

There was more for the young man to behold. As the rockslide moved on, destroying everything in its path, the long railroad trestle that spanned Clear Creek slowly collapsed, folding inward like a construction of matchsticks. Stick by stick, the structure disappeared into a great cloud of smoke and boiling white water at the bottom of the deep canyon.

Thumbs thrust in his back pockets, Will Simpson stared at the wreckage in unabashed pride and awe. It was beyond any daydream he had nurtured during his long, tedious days in the fields of his brother's small farm west of Holbrook, and more vivid than any nighttime fantasy he had created when asleep. *A fine beginning*, he thought proudly. *A fine beginning for the brave, new outlaw Billy Starbuck*.

The restless mule was less enthusiastic. He danced in place, tossing his head and pulling at the reins as he struggled to break free of the young man's grasp. "Not yet," Will whispered, his hand closing across the animal's nose. He squeezed his fingers tight against the mule's flaring nostrils, keeping his hand in place until the beast stopped struggling and was quiet. Firmly, he led the animal out from behind the rocks and back up onto the ruined roadbed, just beyond the section devastated by the dynamite.

A thin plume of white smoke appeared against the western horizon, just around the bend. There was no sound yet, but Will, perched atop one rail like a young eagle, could feel the vibration in the steel beneath his feet. Grinning, he swung up onto the mule's broad back, the rifle still in his right hand.

Gingerly, he urged the mule toward the curve in the tracks, heading toward the smoke. He kept to a leisurely pace, the animal settling into a gentle lope.

And then the engine appeared, sleek black against a cobalt sky, the black smoke at the chimney rising against the blue and turning pure white as it billowed into man-made clouds. Will kept on, using one hand to knot a red handkerchief to the tip of the rifle's hexagonal barrel. He pulled his hat well down on his head, shading his eyes, and then as if he had been sent by Providence, he began to wave his red banner.

Will galloped toward the steam engine, swinging around when the mule came even with the cowcatcher and then adjusting his speed until he was even with the window of the cab. "The bridge is down!" he shouted above the wind and the noise, jabbing the rifle in an easterly direction. *"Bridge down!"* he repeated.

The middle-aged Irishman at the throttle cupped his ear and stuck his head out the window, his red face growing redder as he realized what the young farmer was shouting. There was a flurry of activity inside the cab as the engineer shouted terse orders to his fireman, and then there was the screech and squeal of metal against metal as both men applied their weight against the brake.

Sparks flew as the metal pads pressed against the great wheels. The noise reverberated within the mule's sensitive ears as the engine began to slow down, and the animal began to buck. Will Simpson swore. "Shit!" The mule bucked harder. "Holy shit!"

The steam engine careened closer and closer to the curve leading to the trestle, the curses of the crew loud above the noise, the young man and his mule all but forgotten. And then, finally, the iron horse slid to a stop, no more than a quarter of a mile from the rockslide that had destroyed the trestle across Clear Creek.

As the engineer and fireman leaped from the engine and started to run down the track, Will Simpson fought the mule under control, rewarding the animal's belligerence with a healthy rap between the ears with the barrel of his rifle. The young man's nose was bleeding, and he yanked the red scarf away from the end of the rifle and dabbed at the bright smear above his upper lip. Then, intent on completing his mission, he folded the cloth and tied it across his nose.

Will approached the train, disappointed that in addition to the engine and the tender, there was only one passenger car, and behind that a closed boxcar. He dismissed the boxcar, concentrating instead on the single passenger coach. Easing the mule close to the rear platform, he swung aboard and carefully peered inside.

There were perhaps a dozen people in the small car, almost evenly divided between male and female. Most of the men were on their feet at the opposite end of the car, crowding to get out of the door to see what had happened. Will watched as they departed and followed the engineer up the tracks, a smile touching his lips as he eased through the door.

The remaining passengers—the women and one man—all had their backs to him. They were at the windows, straining to see what was going on, a low murmur filling the car as they expressed their disappointment at being left in the dark. Whatever had happened was up the track and slightly around a small bend. Frustrated, they turned and began to settle back into their seats.

"Ladies," Will Simpson greeted. "Sir." He touched the brim of his hat, his salutation soft and properly respectful.

"Oh, my God," a woman's faint voice murmured as the passengers turned and saw the masked man with the rifle in his hands. For a brief moment, Will was afraid the woman was going to faint.

The insignificant little man in the store-bought suit who had remained behind swore. He was out of his seat, staring hard at the young outlaw who stood before him, his face turning a deep plum color as he suddenly clutched the carpetbag he was carrying to his slack belly. Will saw the panic in the man's eyes and moved forward.

He bypassed the women, shaking his head at an old woman who was struggling to take off and conceal the wide gold band she wore on her left hand. "Don't worry, ma'am," he murmured. His eyes swept her face and then turned to briefly touch the pale countenances of the other ladies. His voice rose slightly. "Billy Starbuck doesn't rob women," he announced, enjoying the sound of his new name and wanting it heard.

"But you, sir," he said. He pointed his rifle at the man's midsection and nodded at the carpetbag. Will's excitement was so intense that he had to suppress a giggle. "Your money or your life!"

The little man recoiled. His eyes swept the quiet band of passive women at the young outlaw's back as if he were asking them for help. He was angry when it didn't come, and the anger prompted a false and righteous courage. "I beg your pardon!" he fumed.

Momentarily taken aback, Billy Starbuck blinked. "The money," he said, gesturing toward the bag the man had tucked beneath his arms. Starbuck tapped it with the barrel of his rifle.

The man laughed. Everything considered, he couldn't help himself. Standing in front of him was a bumpkin with worn-down boots, ragtag clothes, and a small-bore rifle that was little more than a popgun. "You're making a mistake, sonny," he said, shaking his head.

The young outlaw took a single step backward, his blue eyes suddenly becoming ice. He cocked the rifle, careful to keep his words private; ominously he replied, "*You're* making a mistake."

There was a long moment's hesitation as the man considered Billy Starbuck's words, and he felt a bitter irony as he realized what he was going to have to do. He fondled the bag, thinking of the five thousand dollars he had embezzled from his nagging wife's father, knowing there wasn't a damned thing he could do to keep it. His eyes on the cocked rifle, he surrendered his bag—but not without pompous protest. He was already thinking up the lies he was going to have to tell. "Piss-poor way to run a railroad," he groused, his voice rising. "Man can't take a fifty mile ride without being robbed blind, and not one damned bit of help from . . ." The words died.

"Thank you," the young man said politely, taking the satchel. And then, bowing at the waist, he backed away.

Billy moved backward down the narrow corridor, his eyes widening as a young woman on his left smiled coquettishly. She winked, her lips forming a small kiss as she wished him good luck. He touched the brim of his hat and nodded a reluctant farewell.

He had made it as far as the door when some inner sense—some primal instinct—told him that he was in danger. Quickly, he moved away from the door, ducking to one side, his eyes cautioning the passengers to remain silent. The door opened.

"Nothing to worry about, folks," the man crossing the threshold announced. His conductor's cap was perched precariously to one side, and it was obvious from his flushed cheeks that the man had been secreted in the rear car and had been doing a copious amount of drinking. He blustered his way into the coach, assuming the silence that greeted him to be some form of censure that he chose to ignore.

"Going up front myself," he declared officiously. "Take a look-see as to what's going on." He grinned, totally unaware of the young man who was now to his back. "Hell, folks—" his hand went now to his back. "—hell, folks—" his hand went to his mouth "—begging the ladies' pardon, but it ain't like the James boys was here and we was about to be robbed!" He laughed at his own joke and wondered indignantly why the others did not appreciate his brilliant humor.

"Guess again, old man." Billy Starbuck laughed. He tapped the conductor on the back with his rifle and then slid the barrel forward across his shoulder until it extended far enough for the man to see it out of the corner of his eye.

"Oh, damn," the railroad man croaked, not daring to turn around. His slack spine felt like rubber. "You ain't got a chance in hell," he babbled, the words suddenly pouring from his whiskey-glib tongue. "That safe back there," he jerked his head away from the barrel of the rifle and toward the car at his back, "it's made special for the line by some company back east. Ain't a way you're going to get that payroll—not in this lifetime. . . ."

Starbuck silenced the man by simply touching his neck with the cold barrel of the rifle. "We'll just see, old man," he breathed, inwardly pleased at his sudden good fortune.

He pulled the man with him as he backed out of the door, both of them barely fitting into the tight space on the rear platform. Gingerly, Starbuck turned the man in a circle and prodded him forward. The two men stepped across the heavy steel couplers and onto the platform of the almost windowless rear car.

The conductor was sweating. "Just like I told you," he croaked, fumbling with the door. He opened it just slightly, hoping against hope for salvation, disappointed and puzzled when it didn't come.

Standing at the doorway, Starbuck peered over the man's shoulder into the dim interior; the only light came from two high, barred windows at the very rear of the car. Red sawdust littered the floor, and he could make out the distinct shapes of barrels and boxes. And then, at the very rear of the car—illuminated by a silvery shaft of sunlight—Billy Starbuck saw the safe.

It was imposing and clearly built to last. The iron feet, molded in the shape of a lion's paws, were bolted to the floor of the car.

Starbuck prodded the conductor to the edge of the platform with the barrel of his rifle. "Jump down," he ordered, pointing to the gravel roadbed. As if to emphasize his words, he threw the stolen carpetbag in the direction he had indicated. It sailed in a high arc and came to rest in the tall grass beside the embankment. "*Now*," he ordered.

Reluctantly, the railroad man moved. "You listen, fella," he sputtered. And then he shut up. *It will serve the bastard right*, he reckoned. *Let him go inside that car and try to take the safe. Be one surprised little hayseed*. He snorted. *Yes sirree . . .*

The man's joyful reverie was rudely interrupted by the pungent smell of sulfur and the distinctive crackle and sputter of burning fuse. He turned and knew at once that it was too late.

Dropping the spent match, Billy Starbuck tossed the single stick of dynamite inside the car, knowing the satisfaction of hitting his mark as he saw the stick skim across the floor and disappear in the blackness beneath the heavy safe. Still gripping his rifle, he slammed the outer door shut and then leaped from the platform, first slamming his shoulder into the open-mouthed conductor and knocking him to the ground. They rolled and skidded away from the car and down the slight embankment, coming to rest in the long grass.

"Jesus, boy!" the older man sputtered. He was jabbing a rigid finger at the car, spitting grass and gravel out of his mouth as he vainly tried to find his voice. At first Starbuck didn't understand the man's panic. And then he saw.

The large sliding door on the leeward side of the car screeched open, the rusted, metal rollers catching and then refusing to give. Horrified, the young outlaw watched as a man tried desperately to force his way through the narrow opening. One leg first, and then his head and upper torso appeared, as he compacted himself and squeezed through the unyielding barrier—until he was hanging on with just one arm.

Starbuck was on his feet, rifle in hand. Unmindful of the danger, he clambered back up the embankment, knowing the terrible agony of being too late.

The explosion was muted by the compact design of the boxcar. The heavy two-by-six boards, reinforced by steel uprights, billowed outward but refused to yield. Instead, the hanging door and the roof took the full force of the blast. The curved, tar-papered roof was blown completely away, the wood shattering and spiraling up into the air. It began to rain wood, paper dollars, and twenty dollar gold eagles.

Billy Starbuck didn't care. He ran toward the car, an image burned in his mind of a human body being lifted up and out of the now wide-open door.

He found the man on the ground beside the ruined boxcar. Panic gripped Starbuck as he dropped his rifle, fell to his knees, and laid his head against the man's broad chest. The heartbeat was there, remarkably strong and reassuringly regular. Thanking whatever God might be listening, Starbuck straightened, aware of a damp, heavy warmth on his cheek that was fast growing cold. Instinctively, he raised his hand to touch the spot. His fingers came away from his face, covered with blood.

Starbuck stared down at the man who lay beside him, his gorge rising as he realized that the blood on his cheek had come from the man's torn arm and shoulder. Forcing himself, the young outlaw pulled the tattered remnants of the man's jacket away from his body, and felt a sickness deep in his belly as he saw the yellow-white gleam of broken bone.

The women passengers were disembarking from the front end of the passenger coach, their eyes betraying their confusion and shock, their hats akimbo and their faces chalk white. All around them, bouncing against the top of the coach and showering onto the ground, were the gold coins from inside the safe, accompanied by a fluttering cloud of paper currency. The ladies stared up into the heavens, at first frightened by the strange, golden rainfall. Then, recognizing their sudden good fortune, they squealed in delight.

Unmindful of the women who were merrily hunting the gold coins and currency, Billy Starbuck concentrated on the wounded man. He saw the bright red fountain of blood that pulsated just above the man's shattered elbow and knew at once that he was going to bleed to death. "Help me," he croaked, grabbing the arm of the conductor when the man bent down to retrieve a twenty-dollar gold piece that lay beside the injured guard's leg. "Goddammit! Give me a hand!"

The conductor blanched and backed away, as if seeing the blood for the first time. "Christ almighty, Kyle," he whispered, addressing the unconscious man at his feet. Not wanting to look, he stumbled away.

Starbuck hooked his arm around the conductor's boot and rudely dumped him on the ground. When he tried to scramble away, Starbuck straddled him. Unwilling to waste valuable time, he slapped the trainman twice. "I need help with him," he said. "Now!" Without waiting for the man to comply, he yanked the conductor's belt open and pulled it free.

He applied the makeshift tourniquet, wiping the sweat from his chin on his own shoulder as he worked. There was a very real urgency in him as he wound the belt three times around the injured man's arm. "What's his name?" he said, his eyes never leaving the still-spurting flow.

The conductor had regained some of his senses. He worked a thick piece of cloth beneath the belt in a futile attempt to stem the flow. "Lassiter," he breathed, fighting the urge to be sick. "Kyle Lassiter." It seemed a hell of a strange time for an introduction.

Starbuck locked the name into his memory. Desperately, he gave the slippery leather another slow tug, a great sigh coming from him as the flow of blood diminished and finally stopped. "You hold this," he ordered, putting the conductor's pale hand in place of his own as he showed him how to keep the stricture on Lassiter's arm tight. "And you don't let go."

The young outlaw picked up his rifle and rose to his feet. He stared at the destruction around him, amazed and appalled that the main concern of the passengers was with the gold that had fallen from the heavens when the safe gave way. Somehow, thinking of Lassiter, the railroad payroll didn't matter. Not anymore.

A chorus of angry shouts and curses roused Starbuck from his musings. He turned and saw the engineer and fireman pounding down the roadway. Behind them followed the other men who had disembarked from the train to see what had happened at the bridge. The little man robbed by Starbuck inside the train was urging them on. "Thief!" he screamed, pointing an accusing finger at Starbuck. *"Thief!"*

Starbuck headed for the opposite side of the track to the place where he had tethered the mule. He sprinted across the roadway, relieved when he found the animal placidly grazing only a few feet from where he had left him.

He mounted the animal on the run, vaulting up onto his back and urging him across the roadway. He could still hear the rantings of the outraged little man, and when he came back around the end of the car, he saw him—just at the same time the man spotted his stolen carpetbag lying in the grass.

Together, the outlaw and his victim raced toward the prize. The man in the suit was closer, but Starbuck had the advantage of speed. He galloped toward the brightly colored bag, leaning sideways and down as the mule sped by. Swooping up the satchel, he kicked into a full run and headed west toward the mountains.

The young man rode for a long time, the mule dropping into a ground-eating lope that carried him far beyond the trouble and turmoil at his back. And then, when he knew he was safe, he stopped—just long enough to open the carpetbag he had stolen and to count the cash.

Five thousand dollars in paper bills crackled beneath his fingers, the feel of money filling the outlaw with a sense of euphoria that dimmed the memory of his earlier bunglings. He picked up the cash, relishing the texture of it beneath his fingers as he mentally congratulated himself. *Not bad for a short day's work, Will Simpson,* he gloated. And then he shook his head. There wasn't any Will Simpson. Not anymore.

There was no regret in the young man's words and no repentance in his smile. "Billy Starbuck!" he shouted aloud to the world, tossing his hat into the sky. "My name is Billy Starbuck!" He turned, making a slow circle as the mountains echoed his declaration. *Billy Starbuck . . . Billy Starbuck . . . Billy Starbuck . . .*

Chapter Two

Holbrook, Arizona Territory, lay dormant beneath a two-foot layer of compacted snow. The thick, white blanket spread across the mountainous landscape, the terrain rising and falling to merge with the leaden sky on the distant horizon. Nothing but muted shades of dreary gray covered the land that reached into the mists beyond the mountains, where the trestle had been destroyed the previous September by Billy Starbuck.

Simon Tyree swore. He stood in the street beside his coach and team in front of the Navaho Stage Line office, his eyes the same cold gray as the dirty, slate-colored snow beneath his booted feet. "Damn," the senior driver for the stage line muttered. "Goddamn."

He was a tall man, big-boned and bearlike in the heavy fur coat that stretched tight across his broad back. A coiled bullwhip was slung around one shoulder, so much a part of him that it seemed to have grown there.

In his mid-forties, Tyree looked his age, the long winter having robbed him of the dark tan that usually marked his features. His once-bronzed cheeks were red now, burned to a ruddy hue by the same north wind that had stolen the natural moisture from his skin. Even his own breath betrayed him, turning to white hoarfrost beneath his nose and clinging in a layer of ice to his dark mustache.

The wet cold plagued him. A dull, arthritic ache ground at the joints in his fingers, the pain eroding his usually mild disposition until even the most minor irritation set him off.

This time, it was the tardiness of the line supervisor, Carl Demming. Thinking of the man, Tyree cursed again—Demming first and then, with more gusto, the outlaw Billy Starbuck.

Billy Starbuck. Tyree shook his head as he thought of the young outlaw. Single-handedly, he had brought the railroad—the whole territory—to its knees within half a year's time. Because of the trestle and track destroyed by Starbuck in Devil's Canyon, rail service had been shut down between Holbrook and the previous railhead to the west at Flagstaff, from where crews were still extending the westward stretch of track. Until the trestle could be rebuilt later that spring, it was left to Navaho Stage Line to transport passengers, mail, and cargo between Holbrook and Flagstaff—and to deliver the railroad's payroll to its work crews west of Flagstaff once a month. But twice during the long winter, the elusive Billy Starbuck had struck again and had relieved the stage line of its responsibility—by stealing the strongbox containing the payroll.

Unable to help himself, Tyree grinned. Like everyone else, he had at first found the outlaw's bravado more amusing than impressive. The local newspapers were totally responsible for the desperado's current following and reputation. In the beginning, the press had ignored the letters signed by Billy Starbuck claiming responsibility for destroying the trestle and for the two subsequent stagecoach robberies, dismissing the author as some malcontented imposter seeking attention. But later, after he had provided details only the outlaw could have known, his letters began to appear on the front pages, his flamboyant claims adding color to an otherwise drab winter. It was almost as if the press were daring him to continue his war against the local law and the railroad. So now, between Billy Starbuck and the long and unusually harsh winter, nothing much moved between Holbrook and Flagstaff anymore.

Except me, Tyree thought ruefully, no vanity in him as he massaged his sore fingers. It was true; even the newspapers had to admit that where everyone else had failed, Tyree, the senior driver for Navaho Stage Line, had succeeded. Following the two previous stage robberies, the stage line had transferred the veteran driver from another route to handle the trouble-plagued run through Devil's Canyon. The next time the payroll arrived in Holbrook for transport to Flagstaff, Tyree, without even informing his superiors, had picked it up and made an unscheduled run, with only a shotgun guard on board. The bold move apparently had taken Billy Starbuck by surprise, because it resulted in the first on-time, successful payroll run between the Holbrook and Flagstaff railroad offices.

Tyree now intended to make a second—in spite of Billy Starbuck's recently published promise to see that he didn't, and despite Carl Demming's inexcusable tardiness. Impatiently, Tyree dug into his inside coat pocket for his watch. *You've got one minute, Demming*, he thought. *Sixty seconds until I load up the box and leave.*

As if he had sensed the warning, Demming came scurrying across the street. A short, prematurely bald man, he almost lost his footing on the treacherous sheeting of ice that covered the compacted snow, and he called out to Tyree, "You wait, Simon!" The second time, the sharpness left his voice, and he almost seemed to be begging him not to leave. "Simon?"

Out of breath, Demming steadied himself by clutching at Tyree's arm. The driver reached out and lifted the man up off his feet and then held him there, nose to nose, smiling against the pain that coursed through his clenched fingers. "You're late, Carl," he said levelly as he grinned. The smile failed to reach his eyes. "I told you when I agreed to come to this godforsaken hole that if you gave me one minute's grief, I'd leave you to take care of it all. I meant it, Carl."

Demming squirmed free, realizing that it was Tyree's

aches and pains that were making him so cantankerous—
that and Billy Starbuck's letter in that morning's issue of
the *Enterprise*, predicting another successful robbery.

"It's Marshal Thompson," Demming said finally, wisely
avoiding the subject of the outlaw. He took a deep breath
and continued, knowing that his words would not appease
Tyree's temper or improve his disposition. "He's got some
bug up his ass and says you're not to leave until he talks to
you."

Tyree snorted and set the younger man free. "Time,
tide, and Tyree wait for no man," he groused, paraphras-
ing the old proverb. "We've got a contract to honor,
Carl." His voice lowered. "And I've got connections to
make with the military. We're meeting Captain Grant at
Clear Creek after dark." What Tyree neglected to tell
Demming was that the military detail would be transport-
ing the payroll on to Flagstaff that same night, a fact
known only by Captain Grant, the Clear Creek stationmaster, the stagecoach shotgun guard, and Tyree.

Demming shrugged. He nodded his head toward the
coach and the empty seat up top, which the shotgun guard
would fill. "You've got to wait for your shotgunner, Simon," he cajoled. "Maybe Thompson will make it out
here before he does."

Tyree was busy with the harness, the leather ribbons
cold and inflexible beneath his fingers. He pulled off one
glove and fondly scratched the lead bay between the ears.
"Lassiter's minding the store, Carl," Tyree retorted, refer-
ring to the payroll Kyle Lassiter was guarding at the
railroad office. "I'm picking him up at the railroad office
on the way out."

The stage line had recently hired Kyle Lassiter, the
railroad's ace troubleshooter and chief of detectives, who
had lost his left arm to Starbuck's dynamite blast during
the outlaw's first robbery. After recuperating from the
amputation, Lassiter had taken a leave of absence from the
railroad and had hired on as shotgun guard for Navaho
Stage Line, hoping to catch the outlaw in the act of

robbing the railroad's payroll from the stage—and to get his own revenge for the pain and physical loss Billy Starbuck had caused him to suffer.

Tyree felt no great loyalty toward the silent, one-armed guard, but he did respect him for his sense of duty and responsibility. For the past few weeks that he had been working for the stage company, after his long and painful recovery, Lassiter had never been late and was always prepared. Tyree's brow wrinkled as he thought about the man for a moment. There were times, he realized, when Lassiter seemed almost too eager for trouble to come looking for him, *for Billy Starbuck to come looking for him.*

Tyree's dark speculations were interrupted by the distinctive crunch of booted heels against the surface of the frozen street. He recognized the heavy stride of the marshal, Clay Thompson, and turned to greet him.

They shook hands woodenly, and Thompson was the first to speak. His words were as precise and as abrupt as his manner. "Three," he said cryptically. "Three adults and a baby." He indicated a place somewhere behind him with a terse jerk of his head, not even bothering to conceal a smug grin. "You've got passengers this trip, Demming. These folks have been ordered by the court to leave town—" the marshal lowered his voice "—on account of their kind of living arrangement. You've got no choice but to take them." The lawman's last words were directed at the line supervisor, but Thompson's gaze was locked on Tyree's impassive face. He took considerable pleasure in the driver's momentary annoyance.

Demming was shaking his head. "No, Marshal," he said quietly. "We're not taking on any passengers. Not this trip."

"And why not?" Thompson demanded. He gestured toward the coach with his open hand. "You're a transport service, and I got people in need of a ride." The benign smile appeared again, and the lawman lowered his voice in mock secrecy. "Unless you've got some reason for not wanting to haul passengers," he suggested.

Demming's head snapped up. He stared at the marshal, the top of his bald head well below Thompson's chin. He looked like a banty rooster on the prod, puffed up and indignant. "You know goddamned good and well why I don't want to carry passengers this trip," he said evenly, refusing to let the man intimidate him. It was Demming's turn to smile. "We're going to deliver that payroll, Marshal. Simon's going to deliver it, just like he did the last time—*without* your help."

Thompson drew himself up to his full six foot three, his face coloring. "What you're going to deliver—" his eyes lifted until they were squarely, but briefly, fixed on Tyree "—what *Simon's* going to deliver, are the passengers I'm going to make damn sure you carry." He shook a finger at both men. "And I don't give a good goddamn about that payroll!" It was a feeble lie poorly told. It was bad enough that he had been unable to protect first the railroad and then the stage line from a two-bit outlaw like Billy Starbuck, but then this outsider named Simon Tyree had come in and in one bold stroke had managed to evade Starbuck—and without even requesting the marshal's assistance. Tyree and the stage line had made him look like an incompetent fool.

I'm the law, dammit, not Tyree! Thompson fumed silently. *I run this goddamn town—this goddamn county!*

As if he could read the marshal's mind, Tyree snorted and turned back to the horses. The driver had been the first to notice a definite pattern to Billy Starbuck's raids. The outlaw had successfully robbed one train and two stagecoaches before Tyree had realized that all three times the robberies had taken place on the western end of the run, in an area between Devil's Canyon and Flagstaff.

With that realization, Simon Tyree had read and re-read the reports of each robbery and had found something more disturbing than the fact that Starbuck limited his activities to a certain terrain: The outlaw had an uncanny way of knowing not only *where* to strike, but *when*.

Tyree was no fool. He knew that his own success in

getting the last payroll through to Flagstaff was due only to the fact that he had done the unexpected. Rather than wait for the scheduled payroll run, he had met the train at the station and removed the strongbox before the engine ever made the turnaround. And then, without waiting for the usual overnight delay and the audit at the bank, he had simply loaded the box into the Concord and, with a surprised Lassiter in tow, made the run.

His independent move had angered everyone from Marshal Thompson to the railroad's bookkeeper. But most of all, he had surprised and angered—and insulted—Billy Starbuck. It was the first time anyone had outwitted the young outlaw.

The territorial newspapers had a field day when news of the successful payroll delivery was relayed from Flagstaff. The idea of a battle of wits between the seasoned driver, Simon Tyree, and the young robber, Billy Starbuck, generated a great deal of interest and even more publicity.

That was the problem. The newspapers had stuck their noses into railroad business, making a point of publishing everything they could learn about this trip—from the time the shipment was due to arrive in Holbrook to the fact that the bank and Marshal Thompson had demanded a full accounting of the money *before* the stage left with it.

And then they gleefully published Billy Starbuck's latest message, this one a poem. It had been addressed to Simon Tyree and had ended with this bit of doggerel:

> *You fooled me once,*
> *with your plan so bold.*
> *But this time, I promise,*
> *I'll take the gold!*

It was lousy poetry, but it was also a clear challenge. And Tyree had no doubt that Billy Starbuck would keep his word and try to take the payroll.

"You're going to take passengers this run, Demming," Marshal Thompson declared, digging into his coat pocket and pulling out a paper. The growing north wind unfolded the document for the man, and he had to hold it with both hands so that the line supervisor could see.

As Demming skimmed the court order, he swore under his breath. He was shaking, as much from his restrained anger as from the sudden blast of cold. "And just who the hell is going to pay?" he growled, his teeth chattering. Behind him, he could hear Tyree whisper, "*Damn!*"

A second, fierce gust of wind sent all three men scurrying for cover in the Working Man's Saloon, the agreed-upon pickup point for passengers to Flagstaff.

Thompson's passengers were already inside the building. Tyree eyed the quartet. The man, in his late thirties, stood with his arm around a woman young enough, it appeared, to be his daughter. There was an older woman— perhaps the man's age—who stood behind them. A baby was in her arms, and she gazed over its head to meet Tyree's long inspection with a directness that was at once disarming and unsettling. The woman had the most incredible green eyes Tyree had ever seen, and they dominated her face—the kind of face that was enhanced by the subtle changes that come with age.

Demming and Thompson were still feuding, their voices rising as they argued about the fare. Neither man seemed to notice the audience that was gathering around them. The stage line supervisor's voice rose above Thompson's, and he was poking a finger in the marshal's chest as he spoke. "You go to hell, Thompson! The last voucher I took from the county wasn't worth the paper it was written on! No free rides!" he ranted. "Navaho Stage Line doesn't give anyone a free ride." Again, he punctuated the words with a solid poke against Thompson's thick chest.

The lawman had had his fill. He grabbed Demming's hand, his fingers closing around the man's knuckles as he held him in place. "You'll take whatever I give you, Demming. Or you'll find your ass in jail. *My* jail!" He nodded at the small group, still talking about them as if they were pieces of meat. "I want them out of here,

Demming, and so does the judge. *Solomonites*," he added, as if it were a dirty word. "They call themselves Solomonites."

An ominous hush fell over the crowd observing the drama from the bar. And then a low murmur of disapproval and disgust began, the predominately Irish Catholic workmen turning en masse to eye the unwelcome intruders. There was a great deal of bitterness throughout Arizona Territory toward the strange religious sect known as the Prophets of Solomon, with their old-fashioned way of dressing, their strange customs, and their endless evangelizing.

Tyree observed the sudden change in temperament from his place near the door. He stood, his back to the wall, stubborn in his determination to remain aloof from a quarrel in which he had no part. He was not going to take sides, not this time.

A drunken member of a laid-off section crew for the railroad weaved his way across the floor, a warm beer clutched in his beefy right hand. He bypassed Thompson and Demming as if they weren't there, his attentions on the wary travelers. "Harems," he said in a lilting Irish brogue, half turning to wink knowingly at his friends who lined the bar. "They keep themselves a goddamned harem!" His drunken laughter was malicious now, without humor. He spun around suddenly, the beer sloshing across his hand and onto the floor. "Ain't enough decent females to go around as it is, and they take 'em on two, three, at a time!"

The man's bitterness was matched by the mood of the other idle railroad workers who stood drowning their sorrows with stale beer and homemade rotgut. It was a potent political issue, the unwanted presence of the Prophets of Solomon in northern Arizona and their stubborn determination to continue their practice of polygamy. Already, the territorial legislature had taken steps to make the plural marriages a punishable violation of the law. And now, here was another "prophet" come looking for converts in a place where he was not welcome, flaunting two wives in defiance of everything these men considered holy.

The drunk's mood was deteriorating. "Which one?" he breathed, addressing the man.

Josiah Simpson shook his head, not understanding what the man wanted to know. He pulled his young wife even closer, saying nothing, but his silence served only to make the drunk more belligerent. The big Irishman moved closer and reached out, his eyes narrowing as he fingered the lace collar of the younger woman. "Which one is the second wife?" He grinned mirthlessly. "Which one is the whore?"

Elizabeth Simpson, twenty, batted her blue eyes at the big man, who continued to fondle the edging on her dress, not backing away. She was a pretty woman, in the pampered but brainless way of the very young and the very vain, and she canted her head flirtatiously at her unwanted admirer as at the same time she appealed to her husband. "Do something, Josiah," she whimpered. His failure to respond immediately—to do battle for her honor—angered her, and her voice became shrill. "Do something!"

It was Marshal Thompson who finally responded to her plea. With the politician's gift for remembering names and faces, he addressed the young woman's tormentor. "That's enough, Flaherty," he warned.

But Flaherty did not relent. His fingers were still stroking the young woman's collar.

Then the other woman, Rebecca Simpson, handed the child to her husband and placed herself between the younger wife and the intoxicated Flaherty. She faced the big Irishman, wishing that Elizabeth would yield and give her more room at her back. "Leave us in peace," she said quietly. "We intend you no harm and have done nothing to offend you."

Flaherty laughed, the sound coarse and suggestive. "*He* offends me," he snorted, his breath heavy with the stink of beer. "The fact that he has *two* of you offends me." He smiled, shaking his head. "Can't stand a greedy man. Can't stand a man that won't share." He placed a heavy hand on the older woman's shoulder and—obscenely, with a perverted leer on his face—began to move it downward. Roughly, he pushed aside her cloak and groped at her right breast, her dark, high-necked dress somehow more provocative to him than the scanty garb of the saloon whores who stood in a small cluster at his back. Two more men joined Flaherty, goading him on as he continued his exploration of the woman's breast.

Thompson could stand it no longer. Ashamed that he had allowed things to go this far, he tapped Flaherty on the shoulder, hard. He didn't particularly care about the Solomonite and his wives, but he did feel responsible for their safety. "I told you that was enough!" he said sharply.

Without turning around, Flaherty viciously rammed an elbow into Thompson's gut, the glass of beer in his hand wetting his sleeve and the front of the woman's dress before crashing to the floor.

Thompson, the wind knocked out of him, clutched his belly and backed up. In one smooth motion, he drew his pistol and pressed the barrel into the small of Flaherty's back. "Take your hands off her, Flaherty! *Now!*" he ordered.

There was a brief scuffle as the gang of railroad men at Thompson's back jumped into action, their long months of enforced unemployment and confinement fueling a rage that had suddenly found direction. Flaherty was one of their own, and they meant to protect him.

Thompson whirled to confront his attackers. Immediately, he was felled by a single blow to the back of his neck, delivered by Flaherty from behind. He collapsed onto the floor and felt a terrible pain in his wrist as someone kicked the pistol from his hand. Helplessly, he watched as the weapon spun across the floor and disappeared into the crowd of booted feet.

Triumphant, Flaherty turned back to the woman. He grabbed her wrist and pulled her to him, his mouth searching for her lips as one hand pushed aside her cloak. Roughly, his fingers tore at the soft fabric at her neck, ripping her dress to expose her shoulder and the soft, white mound of her right breast. She fought him, not hysterically, but with a minimum of body movement as she attempted to wrench free.

There was a loud *thwack* from somewhere beyond her, and the woman felt the air move near her cheek as a blur of black leather uncoiled and cut through the silence at her ear.

Flaherty screamed and grabbed at his neck with both hands. The black, plaited rawhide whip cut into the thick flesh beneath his fingers, burning his skin. As Simon Tyree pulled the cord tighter with a final, quick flick of his wrist, the Irishman's windpipe compressed.

With expertise, Tyree quickly reeled the man in with the bullwhip, taking advantage of Flaherty's fear and panic. Dispassionately, he turned the man loose, then knocked him down, using the stout handle of the whip as a club. Stunned, the big Irishman fell face forward onto the hardwood floor.

Marshal Thompson retrieved his gun, scrambled to his feet, and pointed the gun at the crowd. He had recovered the weapon but not his dignity, and his anger was obvious in his words. "What the hell took you so long?" he roared, the words directed at Tyree.

Tyree shrugged, nonchalant as he recoiled his whip. "It was between you and them," he declared, nodding at the crowd. "Until that one," he dug at Flaherty's still form with the toe of his boot, "made the mistake of touching one of my passengers."

"Oh, Christ, Simon . . ." Demming whispered. He had hoped that if he argued hard and long enough with Thompson, the line would be spared the responsibility of the unwanted passengers. And now Tyree was making the decision for him. Demming knew that nothing short of an act of God would make the driver change his mind.

Tyree ignored Demming. "We'll take the passengers, Marshal, and we'll take the county voucher," he said. "But when I get back from Flagstaff, you're going to make it good."

Thompson, feeling no gratitude toward Tyree, resented the man's tone. Behind him, the infant began to wail, the noise adding to his consternation. "And if I don't make it good?"

For the first time, Tyree smiled. "Then I'll take it out of your hide," he promised.

There was no doubt in Thompson's mind that he would.

Chapter Three

Simon Tyree followed the Solomonites out of the saloon and down the boardwalk toward the stagecoach, mindful of the mood of the unemployed railroad men behind him. One of them was so close that he could feel the man's breath.

Carl Demming trotted to keep up with Tyree, pressing close to the driver's right shoulder, all the while bemoaning the fact that Tyree had agreed to take the Solomonite and his wives to Flagstaff. "Goddammit, Simon! Do you have any idea what it's like trying to collect on a voucher from the county? My God, man . . ."

Tyree's arthritis was acting up again. "Shut up, Carl," he ordered. "Just shut up!" Right now, the county voucher was the least of his worries. The crowd at his back—their angry mood intensified by their discomfort from the cold—was pressing even closer.

An ominous grumbling began, the obscenities that had been mere whispers growing louder and louder. There was a sharp snap as someone broke off a large icicle hanging from a porch rafter above. The long, dangerously thin piece of ice cut through the air and nicked the side of Tyree's neck. He spun around, facing the mob, his jaws tightening as he searched the area behind them for some sign of the marshal. But Thompson was nowhere to be seen.

Open-mouthed, Carl Demming stared first at the growing crowd and then at Tyree. Already, there was a bright smear of red at the driver's neck, congealing into crystals around the gash. "Oh, Christ," Demming breathed.

Tyree slowly backed away from the crowd, cursing under his breath when they followed him. In such close quarters, the whip was useless, and the single-action Navy Colt he wore in his belt was buried beneath the bulk of his heavy winter coat.

Without turning around, he grabbed the arm of the young woman directly behind him. "Get in the coach," he ordered harshly. "Take the others and get inside the coach." He shoved the woman away, angry when she did not immediately obey. "Now, goddammit!" he roared.

Flaherty pushed forward now, rubbing the back of his head where Tyree had clubbed him. His disposition uglier than before, he stood in front of Tyree, a slow grin creasing his face. In one hand he held a near-empty bottle. Suddenly he flipped the amber bottle into the air, catching it by the neck and smashing it against a hitchrail beside the boardwalk. Sunlight danced off the jagged edges of the bottleneck that remained. "Mine," the big Irishman said, speaking to the men who were clustered at his back. "He's all mine."

Tyree sidestepped the man's thrust, but he felt glass tear through the thick fabric at his belly. Only the heavy coat saved him from being gutted like a pig. He grabbed Flaherty's wrist, and all hell broke loose. The crowd rushed him, a windmill of hands and feet assaulting him, knocking him off the boardwalk to the ground.

The roar of a shotgun boomed above the rumble of voices, the acrid scent of gunpowder heavy in the still air. Tyree scrambled to his feet and backed up, looking to locate the source of the gunshot. He saw Kyle Lassiter on the opposite side of the street, standing beside the stagecoach, a smoking shotgun in his single hand. Nodding to Lassiter, Tyree shrugged his shoulder to free the coiled bullwhip, taking great comfort from the feel of the grip when it slid neatly into his palm. The men who had been pursuing him stopped dead and then retreated in an awkward scramble.

As Lassiter moved to a place just to Tyree's left, he lowered the shotgun, a sawed-off, double-barreled twelve-gauge, until its barrels were nose level with the crowd. He addressed Tyree without looking at him. "I was wondering what was keeping you, so I came over."

"Just in time," Tyree replied. "What about our delivery?"

"It's loaded on board in the strongbox." Lassiter nodded toward the stagecoach. "How come we've got people inside the coach, Simon?" he said quietly. It was clear from his tone that he was not pleased.

"The marshal," Tyree replied. He knew that no other explanation was necessary. "You ready to leave?"

Tight-lipped, Lassiter nodded. "I'm always ready, Simon." This time, there was more censure than displeasure in his words. Clearly, he blamed Tyree for giving in to the marshal about carrying passengers.

Tyree chose to ignore the one-armed man and turned his attention to Carl Demming. "I'll send a wire as soon as we make our delivery." His voice became a whisper. "Get off the street, Carl." He indicated the subdued crowd with a covert nod of his head. "They're still primed for a fight, and once we leave, you're all that's left."

Demming's cheeks were flushed. He had been utterly useless when the cluster of men attacked Tyree, and that truth shamed him. "Thompson should have stopped this," he said finally.

Tyree shook his head. "Thompson's job was finished when I agreed to take the passengers. Get off the street, Carl," he said again. Reluctantly, Demming did as he was told.

Tyree glanced at the sullen men who were gathered on the walkway, and then swung his eyes back to the guard. Lassiter was studying the mob.

There was something about Lassiter that repulsed Tyree. It was not his disfigurement—the scars on his face and the absence of his arm. It was something in the man's eyes, something predatory in the dark orbs, a hunger that Tyree had seen only once before—during the Civil War, when sharpshooters hunted their human quarry like starving men would hunt rats.

Tyree shook the grim thoughts away and turned his attention to the people inside the coach. Although he had not said anything to Demming, the matter of their fare had riled him. It was obvious from their dress and their demeanor that they were well able to afford to pay for their passage. Granted, they were being forced to leave town, but that was none of his doing, any more than it was the fault of the line. They had come to this place knowing they would not be welcome; what had happened as a result was their responsibility. He sure in hell wasn't their keeper.

The older woman was backing out the door when Tyree came around the side of the coach. He stopped midstride, his hands on his hips as he watched her struggle with her skirts. There was something tantalizing in the way she backed down the step, her dress lifting to reveal a trim ankle and a well-turned calf. Tyree's thoughts stopped wandering when the hem of the woman's dress fell back into place. Reaching out, he took her arm and said, "I don't suppose, madam, that you'd care to explain just what you're doing."

Rebecca Simpson's green eyes flashed as she turned to face Tyree. She was tall, almost the same height as he, and her lips were compressed in a tight line. Still staring at him, she lifted his fingers off her arm. "I have a child in there," she began quietly, nodding at the coach. "A child that needs milk, and I intend to get it." She indicated the general store across the street with a nod of her head.

Tyree could not believe the woman was serious. The railroaders were still gathered on the boardwalk, more hostile than they had been in the beginning. He shook his head at her, taking her arm again, his fingers accidentally compressing the soft flesh beneath her cloak when she attempted to pull away. "You can nurse the child," he suggested, embarrassed by a discussion that had somehow become too personal. His eyes swept her as he quickly appraised her manner of dress. "Unless you consider yourself above the commonplace."

"I assure you that if I was able, I would most certainly nurse my husband's child." The anger that moments before had marred Rebecca Simpson's face was now replaced by pain, a sadness that softened the lines at her forehead and misted her emerald eyes.

Tyree was struck dumb, realizing his blunder. The child was not hers. He had seen them together and had assumed that she was the baby's mother—the infant *seemed* to belong to her. Still, his pride kept him from apologizing. Instead, he addressed Kyle Lassiter. "The lady and I are going to take a walk, Kyle. She needs provisions for the child." He could feel the guard's eyes on his back. "You keep an eye on the crowd," he finished. Without another word, he took the woman's arm and began leading her across the street.

Tyree could feel himself being watched—from the coach, by the gaggle of men who stood in the sparse shelter on the boardwalk in front of the stage line office, and covertly by the woman at his side.

And from somewhere else, instinctively, he could feel a pair of hidden eyes watching him.

Will Simpson withdrew into the shadows inside the front door of the mercantile. Broom in hand, he watched as Tyree and his companion approached, a quickening inside his chest as he recognized the pale face of the woman who had been more mother than sister-in-law to him when he was growing up. Half a year had passed since he had last seen Rebecca, but the quiet beauty was still there. She wasn't, of course, pretty in the same way Elizabeth was pretty, but there was a serenity in her that still gave him a sense of home and comfort, a genuine desire for her warm, maternal touch. He hadn't realized until now just how much he had missed her.

His eyes left her and probed the curtained windows

of the coach. He missed Rebecca, but he yearned for Elizabeth. And she was inside that coach. Elizabeth and . . .

Josiah. The mere thought of his elder brother fired the old rage that smoldered at the pit of Will Simpson's belly. He was reminded of the final quarrel between them—as usual, over something inconsequential Will supposedly had done—which had ended with Josiah's attempt to whip him with a leather belt. The very next day Will had decided to follow through with his plan to take his mule, his rifle, and the dynamite used by Josiah to clear large tree stumps, and—as Billy Starbuck—to begin a new life. Even now, as he looked down the street at the stagecoach, he could feel his brother's nearness, the stifling closeness of his disapproving presence.

Will's anger made him careless, and he stood staring out the window until Tyree and Rebecca were already mounting the stairs at the front of the store. Just in time, he propped the broom against the open cracker barrel. "Goin' to the jake, Mr. Tanner," he said, smiling to his employer.

"Fine, Will." The old man nodded and returned the smile. It was a lucky day, the merchant thought, when he had found at his door the young man who called himself only Will. There wasn't a man in town who didn't like his assistant's enthusiasm and willingness to work.

A real go-getter, Tanner mused. Holding down a job here and another as part-time hostler for the stage line.

Yes, he crowed, mentally congratulating himself for keeping such a good worker for such a menial wage. *That Will is a real go-getter.*

Surreptitiously, from the curtained back room, Will Simpson watched as Rebecca selected the supplies she needed. There was, it seemed, a ridiculously long piece of white flannelette being measured out by Tanner, as well as tall stacks of tinned milk and meat and other canned goods that Simon Tyree was collecting from the shelves behind the counter.

It amused Will, seeing Tyree tote and fetch for Rebecca. The senior driver seemed out of place juggling cans of milk and bolts of cloth intended for a baby's rear end.

Will was well acquainted with the driver. The memory of their first meeting brought him a certain perverse pleasure. Will Simpson—*Billy Starbuck*—shaking Simon Tyree's hand! Even now, the memory brought laughter—laughter he was forced to suppress behind a clenched fist.

Tyree's eyes swung to the curtained door at Tanner's back. He stared at the faded draperies for a time, his eyes narrowing as he caught a subtle movement behind the cloth. His left hand disappeared beneath his coat, and he addressed Tanner in a low voice. "Who's in the back room, Sid?"

Tanner felt no real need to look. "Must be Will. Probably left the back door open." As if a sudden blast of wind had chilled him, he shuddered. "Forget his head if it wasn't nailed on," he groused.

Well acquainted with Tanner's penchant for complaining—and not wanting to be drawn into a long, one-sided conversation—Tyree only nodded. It was a plausible explanation. He'd had it out with Will that very morning himself. He had caught the young man in the front office playing telegrapher's helper when he should have been outside helping with the team, and he had chewed him out accordingly. The memory evoked a smile. Will certainly seemed to be interested in everything.

Rebecca Simpson had finished her shopping. As Tanner loaded the supplies in a canvas sack Rebecca had brought, she paid the bill, counting out the exact amount in copper and silver coins, and then she was ready. "I have the things I need, Mr. . . . ."

"Tyree," the driver told her. "Simon Tyree."

Rebecca nodded. "And I'm Rebecca Simpson, traveling with my husband Josiah and with . . . with Elizabeth. And thank you," she finished, wanting to make peace.

Tyree was in no mood to exchange pleasantries. His joints were beginning to ache again, and the clock on the far wall reminded him that he was well behind schedule. "Then let's go," he said, picking up the sack and hoisting it onto his shoulder. When the woman hesitated, he snapped his heels together and made a grossly theatrical bow. "*Now*, madam," he intoned, thinking that she had a lot of nerve for someone who was getting a free ride.

Green eyes blazing, Rebecca swept past the driver, pausing only long enough to relieve him of his burden. She carried the sack as though it contained duck down, determined to let the man know her need of him was only temporary. And then, angry, she stopped in her tracks before exiting from the mercantile and whirled around so abruptly that Tyree collided with her. She stood her ground, refusing to let the man's closeness intimidate her. "How much?" she whispered, choosing to keep these words between them.

Toe to toe with the woman, Tyree remained rooted to his spot. "How much *what*?" he asked.

"For our tickets," she replied. She saw the startled look of confusion on Tyree's face and smiled coldly. "I asked you a question, Mr. Tyree."

"Thirty dollars," he replied, quickly ciphering in his head. This woman had an uncanny ability to know what was on his mind.

Still holding the sack, she managed to dig into her purse, her eyes never leaving the driver's face. Deftly, she chose the coins by feel, withdrew them, and taking the man's hand in her own, doled them out one by one. Three ten-dollar gold pieces, the remainder of what she had earned teaching school before they had left for Holbrook to begin their work as missionaries. "We owe you nothing, Mr. Tyree. Nothing." She smiled with an aura of self-satisfaction. "But *you*, Mr. Tyree, owe my husband and our family all the courtesies normally extended to paying passengers." She dropped the sack and made a quick curtsy. "You may carry my bag now, Mr. Tyree."

Silently cursing, Tyree picked up the sack the woman had dropped on his foot. He started after her, only to have the door slammed in his face. Somehow, he had the uncomfortable feeling that it was going to be a long trip.

*   *   *

Will Simpson stepped out of his hiding place, seemingly nonchalant as he crossed the room and resumed his sweeping. From his vantage point at the frost-covered window, he could make out Tyree and Rebecca, and beyond them Kyle Lassiter.

The sight of Lassiter's pinned-up coat sleeve caused the young man to shudder. A twinge of remorse about the guard's injuries tugged at him and then just as quickly evaporated. After all, Will had had no idea Lassiter had been hiding in that baggage car. And hadn't he saved the injured man's life by his quick action, at the risk of his own safety? Will further consoled himself with the memories of the other good things he had done after the railroad guard was hurt: the personal letters he had sent Lassiter, the money to pay his medical bills.

A glimpse of Elizabeth as Tyree opened the door of the coach roused the young man from his self-righteous indulgence. He could see her small face, the curve of her forehead, and the ringlets that framed her eyes. He loved her; he had always loved her. And he loved their child.

The thought of the baby brought a stab of pain and envy. He wanted the baby, almost as much as he wanted Elizabeth. And he was going to take them.

He laid the broom aside, watching after the coach as it began to move out. "Mr. Tanner," he called, still staring out the window. "I'm going to have to leave early, Mr. Tanner." He turned then to look at the man, a smile forming on his lips and lighting his blue eyes.

Tanner snorted indignantly. His expression changed as he looked around the room and saw that the young man had finished with his sweeping. Feeling benevolent, he dug into his pocket and tossed him a silver dollar. "Don't you go spending that all in one place, Will," he advised.

Will Simpson turned the coin over and over between his thumb and forefinger, thinking of the twenty-dollar gold pieces stuffed in his pants pocket. "No, sir," he said appreciatively. He put the coin into another pocket and patted it, knowing that very soon it would be joined by a great many others. "No, sir!" he repeated. And then he was gone.

Chapter Four

The road leading out of Holbrook was little more than two wheel ruts divided by a deep furrow cut into the compacted snow by the shod hooves of heavy dray animals. The horses followed the path now, moving at a slow walk. The trip to Flagstaff—which during the summer was a thirty-hour run with a change of horses every twenty-five miles—now required a full two days and a stop every twelve miles for a fresh team.

Simon Tyree cursed the lateness of the hour. The long delay in Holbrook had been compounded by an injury to the lead gelding. Ice had lodged against the tender pad in the center of the animal's right front hoof, bruising it and laming the horse, slowing the team to a soul-wearying walk.

Kyle Lassiter had dozed off. By now accustomed to the rigors of outdoor living, he slept sitting up, his hat pulled low over his eyes. The even drone of his light, regular snores added to the mesmerizing spell of the horses' pace, and Tyree found it more and more difficult to stay awake.

There was little to relieve the tedium of the dull landscape. The dying sun had failed to break through the gray mists rolling down from the mountains. Looking down from his perch on the driver's seat, Tyree felt that everything was conspiring to put him at ease, from the soft jingle of the harness hardware to the measured up-and-down working of the animals' rear ends. It would be so easy, he realized, to yield to the deceptive calm and simply go to sleep.

"And freeze to death," he muttered. His voice seemed unusually loud, and he cast a sidewise glance at Lassiter to see if it had roused him.

The guard stirred only slightly and shifted in his seat. His head lolled back, shifting his hat and revealing his face. Even at rest, the man had the wary look of a hunter about him. There was nothing relaxed in his expression, no easing of the grim set of his mouth.

Tyree forced himself to think about all the things he had heard about Lassiter. Everyone in the territory knew the story. Starbuck's enthusiasm for using dynamite had not been matched—in the beginning—by any degree of expertise. During the first robbery, the outlaw had not only blown up a safe and a boxcar, but to the delight of the passengers had salted the surrounding countryside with twelve thousand dollars in paper currency and gold coin.

It was a small miracle that only Lassiter had been injured. The newspapers—the same tabloids that later began to print Billy Starbuck's writings—had made a big deal about the way the gallant young desperado had risked capture by remaining behind long enough to tie off Lassiter's shattered arm and instruct the conductor on what to do.

Tyree was startled as Lassiter bolted awake. It was as if the man were aware of his thoughts and had chosen to interrupt them before Tyree could intrude any longer in his constant nightmare. The guard's eyes were cold and unseeing at first, still clouded by the scenes that had danced behind his closed lids, and he looked at Tyree as if seeing someone else—someone he wanted dead.

Tyree reached out, his fingers closing on Lassiter's wrist before the man could raise the shotgun. There was a tense moment before awareness touched Lassiter's brown eyes and his sensibilities returned. Tyree let go. "Bad dream, Kyle." It was more a statement than a question.

Lassiter smiled, and his eyes narrowed. The fingers of

his right hand were stroking the barrel of the shotgun.
"Not for me," he said quietly.

He had dreamed Billy Starbuck dead, and the feeling
was still with him, as if the heavens were giving him a
sign. *This trip*, he thought. *I'll get him this trip*.

And then the nightmares would stop. The long, tor-
turous dreams where rats gnawed at his bones and ate
away his arm.

Will Simpson—Billy Starbuck—pulled the small black
mare to a halt at the base of a solitary telegraph pole well
outside Holbrook. He sat still for a time, patting the
horse's well-muscled neck, exhibiting an easygoing affection for the animal. The mare, along with a new rifle and
set of clothes more befitting a dashing young desperado,
had been purchased with the money taken in the first
robbery. For a few moments, Starbuck contemplated his
next move. And then, gingerly kicking his feet out of the
stirrups, he hoisted himself up and stood on the saddle.

A linesman's belt was looped over his shoulder. He
worked it free, refastening the strap around his thin waist.
Then he wrapped a leg around the pole and deftly shin-
nied his way up to the top. The young man secured
himself with the belt, no fear in him as he set about
splicing the wire and patching in a portable telegraph key,
which hung from the belt. He was humming, going about
his business as if it were a daily event, totally unconcerned
about the height or the sway of the tall pole.

Billy Starbuck was intelligent—perhaps too intelligent. He possessed an almost photographic memory, and
his ability to mimic what he had seen was uncanny. There
had been only one occasion when he had actually observed a telegraph linesman at work, but that one time
had been enough. He had mastered the art of splicing and
patching into an open line as easily as he had mastered the
telegraph code itself.

The portable key, like the linesman's belt, was part of
the varied collection of booty that he had taken over the
previous few months. Everything had a use, he reminded

himself again and again: if not now, then sometime in the future.

The connection made, Starbuck tapped out his message. It was short and to the point, using the prearranged password Simon Tyree himself had originated.

The first message went to the company of cavalry bivouacked at Camp Sunset. Efficiently, he sent the missive: *Unexpected twenty-four-hour delay due to change in plans. Will rendezvous at Clear Creek accordingly. Tyree.*

Patiently, Starbuck waited for his answer. It came: an unquestioned acknowledgment of his request. There would be no troopers waiting to meet the stage at Clear Creek when Tyree arrived.

Smug and satisfied, the young outlaw sent his second dispatch, this time to the stationmaster at Clear Creek. It was almost the same as the first: *Unexpected twenty-four hour delay. Will rendezvous with stage at Clear Creek accordingly. Franklin Grant, Captain, U.S. Cavalry.* Again, the acknowledgment came. There was no reason for anyone to question either transmission.

Starbuck repaired the line, severing the connection he had made. And then, thinking twice, he cut the line again and left it hanging loose.

Recklessly, using the belt, the young man crow-hopped quickly down the pole. Accurately judging the distance, he unfastened the strap and swung outward as he neared the bottom, dropping neatly into the saddle. He turned the mare and kicked her into a run, his voice lifting in a triumphant parody of an Apache war cry. There would be no military waiting for Simon Tyree at Clear Creek, just as there would be no military to take and transport the railroad payroll in secret to the bank at Flagstaff.

Thirty miles northwest of Holbrook, Simon Tyree pulled his team to a slow walk. He cursed, angry at the cloud-filled sky that hid a full moon. There was almost no light now, and the world was suddenly a place of harsh, deceptive black shadows that stretched across the snow.

The lack of light spooked the horses, and they came

to a complete halt, dancing in their traces as Tyree attempted to urge them on, swearing. Their ears swiveled forward and back as they sensed strange noises from all around them—the distant cry of a nighthawk, the subtle popping of frozen bark from trees that seemed to be breathing. Even the air was different.

Tyree's voice lifted in yet another stream of lyrical curses, swearing at the weather this time. He had sensed the change in the air even before the horses. The bulky fur coat he was wearing was suddenly too warm . . . just as the wind that touched his cheek was too warm.

Patiently, he again urged the animals forward, his voice a soothing singsong as he called out to the lead mare.

"Easy, Sheba," he cajoled. The horse responded, and now he could feel the leather ribbons beneath his fingers yielding to the mare as she once more put her weight against the heavy harness, the other horses following her lead. There was a wet sound as their hooves broke through the thick crust of ice and they began to plow through a thick layer of newly formed slush.

The wet sound, so different from the noise of iron shoes striking ice and packed snow, alarmed Tyree. Clear Creek was still ahead of them, and beyond that, Devil's Canyon Creek, the small tributary of the Little Colorado, which snaked its way through Devil's Canyon. In the frozen grip of a long winter, or during the hot and dry summers, the small rivers proved no challenge for the sturdy Concords that traversed their broad expanses. It was in the spring, during the sudden thaws brought on by the warm *vientecitos*—the little winds from the south— that the crossing proved treacherous, even deadly.

And Tyree had just felt the kiss of the warm winds of a false spring against his face. "It's too soon," he muttered.

"Huh?" Lassiter came fully awake, the shotgun poised at the ready in the crook of his right arm.

"We've got trouble, Kyle. It's getting warm," he said. "Can't you feel it?" Without another word, he uncoiled the big whip. The thick, black leather thong disappeared into the darkness, the loud crack exploding from the tip, directly between the heads of the two lead horses.

"You worry too much, Simon," Lassiter chided as he braced himself for the sudden forward lurch he knew would come as the horses started to run. It was a strange admonition from a man who rode guard with his forefinger curled around the trigger of his shotgun.

Tyree was too concerned about the change in the weather to answer. He called out to the horses, urging them on, relieved when the coach picked up speed. They were on a downward course now, well into the subtle decline that led to Clear Creek and the crossing.

The shimmer of solid ice greeted them as they rounded the final curve, and the horses sensed the nearness of the way station across the river. Sheba, the big lead mare, called out in greeting. Out of habit and in unison, the horses slowed their pace and went easily out onto the frozen river. They crossed the ice without incident and, of their own accord, pulled to a stop directly in line with the front door of the way station, right between the house and the place where the fresh team should have been standing, harnessed and waiting.

Tyree's eyes searched the darkness in front of the house and then swung to the fenced-in lean-to attached to the main house. Confused, restless, the fresh team milled about beneath the thatched shelter.

Lassiter spoke first. "The horses," he began, watching as Tyree climbed down from the driver's box. "Where the hell are the horses? And where's that detail from Camp Sunset?"

Tyree said nothing. Instead, he climbed back up from the ground until he was eye level with the guard, at the same time pulling his rifle from its place beneath the seat. "Stay here, Kyle, until I see what's going on." He didn't wait for an answer.

"Parsons!" Tyree called. When there was no response, he shouted the stationmaster's name again and cocked the rifle. "Parsons!"

There was a slight pause, and then came the sound of

the front door being pulled open. "Wake the dead," Parsons groused. He stood at the threshold, the light at his back as he tucked in his shirttails. "Well, come in, Simon!" he ordered. "I'm not about to stand here and freeze my ass off waiting!"

Tyree remained in the shadows, just to the right of the front wheel. "The team, Owen," he said softly. "Where is the fresh team, and the detail from Sunset?"

Parsons scratched himself and swore. "Tomorrow," he barked, as if talking to a simpleton. "Came over the telegraph. Your soldier boys won't be here until tomorrow!" Disgusted and cold, the man dismissed Tyree with an abrupt wave of his hand and slammed the door.

Tyree uncocked the rifle. There was a tight feeling deep in his gut, and the cramping extended around to the small of his back. Something was terribly wrong. "We're going inside, Kyle," he said finally.

The door on Tyree's side of the coach opened, and a woman called out, "Mr. Tyree?"

Tyree had all but forgotten his unwanted passengers. He made no effort to hide his displeasure. "We'll be spending the night," he said, as if it were the woman's fault. And then, repentant, he reached up and offered her his arm.

She accepted his offer, her words intentionally sarcastic. "How gallant."

Impulsively, Tyree changed his tack. He withdrew his arm, instead reaching up and placing both hands around the woman's small waist. Bodily, he lifted her down from the coach, surprised at how little she weighed. He held her for a time at eye level, her feet just barely above the ground.

Rebecca Simpson's face drained of color, and then just as quickly, her cheeks flamed a bright red. And yet she did not pull away, even when Tyree set her firmly on the ground. There was a long awkward moment between them, and she was momentarily speechless. She recovered her voice and her composure at the same time. "Thank you," she murmured and then curtsied away.

For the first time in the long day, Tyree smiled. "My pleasure," he answered truthfully. Somehow, the unplanned overnight stop had lost some of its dreariness.

Lassiter brought the driver back to the here and now. "I don't like it, Simon. I want to know *why*." Kyle's mood was as grim as ever. Without waiting for Tyree's response, he headed for the station door.

Tyree followed in his wake, aware that his passengers were behind him. He mentally cursed the sweet, lavender scent of the tall woman directly behind him for causing his lapse of reason a moment before. He was almost glad when the infant she was carrying began to wail.

From inside the house, Tyree could hear the loud rantings of Owen Parsons. "Passengers! Jesus Christ, didn't nobody say nothing about any damned passengers—not this trip!" He paused in his complaining just long enough to slam a pot down onto the stove and then swore again when he heard the whimperings of the child. "A baby! Jesus Christ, a baby!"

Tyree held the door open, standing back as the passengers trooped inside. "Josiah Simpson," he said, speaking to the stationmaster. He half turned, his eyes meeting Rebecca's as the rest of the introduction died on his tongue. Not wanting to cause the woman any more pain or embarrassment, he continued, "And his family." There was no reason to give Parsons another reason to continue his loud and thoughtless complaining.

Will Simpson was on his way to the place where Billy Starbuck lived—where he kept Billy Starbuck hidden.

He had found the abandoned log cabin in late autumn of the previous year, during the long days when the sun ruled the land and when the water in the small river was still warm enough for afternoon swims. It sat on a small rise above the creek, in the black depths of Devil's Canyon, the back wall nestled firmly against the base of a high cliff. Now, in the midst of a harsh winter, the building was nearly hidden by the deep snow.

It was clear from the cabin's neat appearance that

Starbuck was not afraid of hard work. He had spent considerable time alone there, attending to the necessary outside repairs and then using the slag that was scattered about the site to patch the flagstone fireplace and hearth within.

The young outlaw felt a great sense of self-satisfaction every time he stepped through the doorway. The furnishings were simple, built to endure the rigors of daily use. A small table sat in the center of the room, directly in front of the fireplace, the matching benches carefully tucked out of the way beneath. Along the wall opposite the fireplace was a narrow bed, with built-up sides and drawers in its base. Starbuck had replaced the mouse-eaten mattress with simple straw-filled ticking covered with a dark buffalo robe that he had pilfered in Holbrook from Simon Tyree's coach.

A second buffalo robe hung from wooden pegs on the back wall of the single-room cabin, the immense hide almost covering the wall. A fat-cheeked pack rat peered out from behind the buffalo skin, his head disappearing briefly as the trail-worn young outlaw came through the door and stomped the snow off his boots. Impudently, the animal poked its nose out a second time. The rat screeched its indignation, more angry than frightened, when the young man continued to stamp his feet.

"Booger!" Starbuck laughed. He scooped up a mass of wet snow from the floor, rolled it into a ball, and chucked it at the animal. The cold missile was purposely thrown high, and it hit the stretched hide well above the small rat's head, a dull *thump* sounding as the hide reverberated like the skin of a gargantuan drum. The pack rat's shrill cry faded as it disappeared behind the robe a final time.

Starbuck crossed the floor hurriedly, lighting and then picking up a small kerosene lantern from the table, pausing only long enough to lift up one corner of the heavy buffalo robe. Then, stepping up and over the bottom two logs that formed the base of the wall, the young man disappeared into the dark, secret cavern that stretched beyond the confines of the cabin's front room.

The outlaw had discovered the cavern quite by acci-
dent, with the help of the same pack rat that now scurried
ahead of him. Starbuck never failed to show his apprecia-
tion to the little animal. Hanging the lantern on a peg, he
dropped to one knee, dug into his coat pocket, pulled out
a handful of shelled corn, and fed the small beast.

He took his time feeding the animal, talking to it as if
it understood, as if it could be trusted. "Big money," he
said, grinning. "Old Simon's carrying close to twenty-five
thousand dollars this trip. Damndest thing," he went on,
scratching the rat behind the ears. "They're going to carry
the box just as far as Clear Creek Station and then let the
military have it!" The young man laughed, his tone growing secretive. "That's because Billy Starbuck," he continued, thumping his chest, "never makes his move until the
coach is somewhere between Devil's Canyon and Flagstaff!"

The observation sobered the young man. It was careless not to have realized he had been making moves that
other men could assess and ultimately anticipate. It was a
weakness that could render him vulnerable and make him
an easy target for a man like Kyle Lassiter.

Or Simon Tyree, Starbuck mused. He was more concerned about Tyree than he had ever been about Lassiter.

His mind busy, Starbuck scattered the last few ker-
nels of corn on the floor. It was getting late, and he had
things to do.

Carefully, the young man changed his clothes. He
kicked out of the round-toed shoes he wore in town and
then laid aside his flannel shirt and coveralls. A strange
transformation seemed to take place as he changed into
the neatly creased, black whipcords. A dark, shield-front
shirt topped the belted trousers, a pair of high-heeled
boots with silver spurs completing the outfit. There was
nothing sissified about the young outlaw or his dress. It
was as if he had stepped out of one of the intricate pen-and-
ink drawings that illustrated the tales of Black Bart and
Jesse James.

Only the revolvers were missing, the pair of deadly
Colts that all the dime-novel Robin Hoods wore. The only

weapon Billy Starbuck carried was his Winchester Centennial repeating rifle—the one vanity he had allowed himself.

Smoothing his fair hair into place, he put on a black, flat-crowned Stetson, pausing only long enough to remove the black silk scarf he had kept tucked inside. Knotting the handkerchief around his neck, he stood back, examining his image in the cracked mirror that hung on the rough wall of the dark cavern. "The last time," he said softly. "This will be the last time."

He was thinking of Elizabeth again—Elizabeth and their child—and of the life they would have together after he took Simon Tyree's strongbox.

Twenty-five thousand dollars, he thought. It would be a fitting dowry for the woman he intended to take as his bride.

Chapter Five

The way station at Clear Creek had suffered through many past lives and now had been reincarnated once again as a temporary stopover for Navaho Stage Line's run between Holbrook and Flagstaff. A sturdy dwelling fashioned out of pine logs and flagstone, the eighteen-by-twenty-four-foot cabin was divided into a large living room and two small bedrooms, none of the three rooms bespeaking any degree of elegance. It was clearly a man's domain, suited to a man's simple needs—Owen Parsons's simple needs.

It was also, by a woman's standards, filthy—and young Elizabeth Simpson lost no time in making known her displeasure with the accommodations.

Rebecca Simpson watched as the old man fussed and fumed over the old cast-iron cookstove. She had sensed his animosity as soon as they had entered the room and was at first put off by his rudeness and his constant grousing. In his seventies, Parsons was lean and bent, his gnarled, painful joints silent testimony to a hard life. Looking at him, Rebecca now sensed something poignant beneath his rough veneer: He was as much embarrassed as he was put out by their presence.

Silently, without being noticed, Rebecca left the cabin. Drawing her cloak up around the shoulders of her torn dress, which she had roughly repaired during the stage ride, she went to the coach.

She had been wise in her selection at Tanner's store in Holbrook. Not only had she purchased food and milk for the baby, but she had had the foresight to stock up on a supply of canned goods and meat, including a cured ham. She and Josiah had been forced to move on before; it had been a difficult experience the first time, and the woman had vowed she would never be caught unprepared again.

Rebecca returned to the cabin as quietly as she had gone out. Setting the food down, she crossed the room, shedding her cloak as she moved. "Mr. Parsons," she began.

The old man either could not or did not want to hear her. She tried again, raising her voice only slightly. "Please, Mr. Parsons." This time he turned to face her. "My mother taught me that only an ungrateful or an ill-bred guest would intrude on a man's house without bringing her own stores." She smiled, gesturing to the bag she had set down. "I'd consider it a kindness if you would allow me to fix supper."

Parsons stood, mouth agape, staring into the woman's green eyes. Her smile was real, and he returned it. "Well now, missy," he began.

Rebecca reached out, touching his arm. "Please, Mr. Parsons," she said again. There was nothing condescending or patronizing in her tone.

Parsons nodded, his smile growing. It had been a long time since a woman had cooked for him, and even longer since one had treated him as anything more than a servant or with any real degree of respect. He handed her the heavy metal spoon he had been using as a scraper and backed away, disappearing into one of the bedrooms and shutting the door.

Rebecca rolled up her sleeves. She used a poker to lift the heavy lid on the water reservoir on the side of the stove and was disappointed when she found only a thimbleful in the bottom. In order to cook a meal she would first have to wash the dishes, and in order to do that . . .

She sighed. And then she bent down to pick up the big enamel pail.

A gloved hand closed around her small fingers. Simon Tyree's face was only inches from her own when she lifted her head. "Snow," she began, feeling foolish, "to melt for water."

"And wood for the fire," he answered. Gently, he uncurled her fingers from around the wooden handle on the pail. Across the room, the child began to whimper. "You take care of the baby. I'll see to the stove and the water." Without another word, he left her.

It took eight trips outside before Tyree was done. He finished stoking the fire just as the baby emptied the last of its bottle. He watched as Rebecca cleaned the child's face and bottom and then surrendered it to Elizabeth and Josiah, who were seated beside the long dining table.

"Why?" he asked when Rebecca returned to the stove.

Rebecca ladled out just enough tepid water to wash the dishes she would need for their evening meal. The pots would be first, so that their dinner could cook while she did the rest of the cleaning. She was already drying the big Dutch oven when she responded to Tyree's question. "Why what, Mr. Tyree?"

The driver took a piece of the new flannel she had brought in and began wiping the heavy cast-iron skillet she had just washed. "Why do you do her work for her like that?" He made little effort to hide the contempt in his voice for the young woman, Elizabeth, who behaved like a pampered princess.

Rebecca's eyes lowered as she scoured the last bit of grit from a smaller skillet. "She's been sick," she answered finally.

Tyree snorted. "Since about six months before the baby came, no doubt. And your husband," he went on—it galled him how the man had remained sitting on his duff even when Rebecca had been about to go out for the snow she needed to melt for water—"how long has he been sick?"

Rebecca's head came up, a fire lighting her green

eyes. The sweat-damp auburn hair at her forehead had begun to form little ringlets, and they framed her face in a way that made her even more attractive. "Josiah's concerned about Elizabeth," she whispered.

Without knowing why he was doing it, Tyree continued to badger the woman. "And *you*, Mrs. Simpson? Is he ever concerned about *you*?"

Rebecca turned from him, her teeth digging into her lower lip as she fought a sudden urge to cry. It was hard enough, sharing Josiah with Elizabeth, without having someone remind her just how little her husband seemed to care about her now. "It's none of your business, Mr. Tyree!" she raged in a barely contained whisper as she whirled to face him. "Whatever there is between my husband and me, between Elizabeth and me, it's none of your business!"

Tyree was surprised by the woman's quiet vehemence. He had seen one example of her spirit when they were together in Tanner's store, and it pleased him to see that same fire again, although subdued. *God, she's beautiful,* he thought, seeing the flash of color in her pale cheeks. "I'm sorry," he said.

Rebecca nodded her head, saying nothing. With his help, she began to prepare their supper.

The entire cabin seemed to fill with the good smells that emanated from the stove. There was the tart sweetness of cinnamon, brown sugar, and fried apples, blending with the aroma of ham and fried potatoes, and the equally pleasing scent of baking-powder biscuits.

Owen Parsons came back into the room, lured by the smell of dinner. He had put on a clean shirt and was wearing a threadbare jacket that matched, but was considerably darker than, his faded trousers, and he had combed his white hair. Rebecca noted the change with the same quiet grace that had marked their first short conversation. Smiling, she pulled out the bench at the head of the table. "Mr. Parsons," she greeted him, patting the rough seat. Proudly, the old man took his place.

They all sat, Josiah taking it on himself to pronounce

the blessing. Tyree interrupted him. "This is Parsons's house, Simpson," he said quietly. He did not care one way or the other about Josiah Simpson's religious beliefs, but he did resent the way the man assumed he could impose those beliefs on others.

There was a tense moment as the two men exchanged a harsh, silent glare. Young Elizabeth spoke up, piously chiding her husband. "He *is* right, Josiah," she began. She was well acquainted with her husband's long-winded prayers. "And if Mr. Tyree chooses to be ungodly, then . . ."

Tyree silenced her with a single look. "I'm simply pointing out that this is Parsons's house and his table," he intoned.

Parsons, clearly enjoying the flurry of attention, smiled and then bowed his head.

Tyree took a deep breath, unsure as to what to expect. He had known Parsons for many years, and not once in all that time had he heard the old man utter a single word that could be considered reverent. To the contrary, the old reprobate delighted in reciting, at the drop of a hat, every bawdy limerick he had ever heard.

Parsons was seated next to Rebecca and must have sensed her discomfort at the confrontation, for he decided to repay her kindness in kind. "For what we are about to receive, Lord," he murmured softly, "for what we are about to share, let us be truly thankful."

The food eased the tension that had dominated the room moments before. Elizabeth no longer whined and complained about her accommodations and displayed, Tyree thought, a healthy appetite. Even a humbled Josiah Simpson made an attempt at general conversation, and soon he and Kyle Lassiter were deep in a discussion of their experiences in the Civil War.

Tyree listened, ever the quiet observer as he lingered over a final cup of coffee. His meal sat heavy and uneasy in his belly; he was unable to shake the feeling that something was wrong.

He reviewed his original plan, carefully recalling every detail. It had been his idea to call on the military for assistance. He had sent a wire to Captain Grant himself and then had made the long ride alone to Camp Sunset to complete the arrangements.

They were to have a rendezvous here at the Clear Creek station, Tyree transferring the strongbox containing the railroad payroll to a detachment of six troopers, who would then transport the gold to the bank in Flagstaff, via the back trail. Tyree and Lassiter would continue their run as if they still carried the box, knowing that somewhere between Devil's Canyon and their destination, Billy Starbuck would make his move.

Tyree's brow wrinkled as he stared into his half-empty coffee cup. He could not understand the failure of Grant's cavalrymen to show up. Something didn't feel right about the delay.

"More coffee, Mr. Tyree?"

Rebecca's voice came to him as if from somewhere far away. He looked up, staring into her eyes. The coffeepot was poised in one hand, her other arm holding the wide-awake infant, balanced against her left hip. Tyree's eyes swept the room, and he saw that Josiah and Elizabeth had already retired. Lassiter was gone as well.

He reached up, taking the pot from Rebecca's hand. "You look like you need it more than I do."

Rebecca laughed, and it was a good sound. "Just one cup," she sighed, sitting down. There was so much to do. The table hadn't been cleared, and the baby had not yet been bathed.

Tyree watched as she perched the child on the edge of the table. It was the first time that he had bothered to take a really good look at the infant. "How old?" he asked softly. He touched the child's fat belly and felt a small hand curl around his fingers.

Rebecca's eyes shone with pride, a different kind of warmth in them than the blaze he had seen earlier when she had lost her temper. "Eight months. Look," she said, inserting a finger gently inside the baby's mouth. He chewed greedily on her finger, a wet laugh bubbling up from between the gleaming white nubs that sprouted from his gums. "Two on top, two on the bottom, and he's already cutting more!" she announced proudly.

Tyree patted the baby's smooth cheek. "What's his name?"

Rebecca's hand was busy forming a curl at the top of the little boy's head, the blond hair winding neatly around her finger. "Benjamin," she said, smiling.

"Benjamin," Tyree repeated. "He who is full of promise. You've got a lot to live up to, trooper!" His fingers traced the baby's features, trailing across his cheek to his pug nose. The boy followed the man's moves with his wide, blue eyes, and they crossed when Tyree's finger reached the end of his nose. Both Rebecca and the driver laughed. The child hesitated and then joined them, his laughter low and almost raucous—as if someone had told him a particularly racy joke and he had understood.

Succumbing as much to the baby's laughter as to the woman's joy, Tyree reached out. The little boy mimicked his move and fell forward into the man's awkward embrace.

"Aha!" Rebecca laughed. She shook a finger at Tyree. "Dogs and children . . ."

He pretended not to understand, as if he didn't know the old saw about hounds and kids and their supposed inborn ability to judge a man's true nature. "I hate dogs," he lied. The baby was playing with his nose.

"Of course," Rebecca replied knowingly. Inwardly, she was amazed at Simon Tyree's exhibition of tenderness toward Benjamin. It was so unlike what she had seen earlier, when he had faced the men from the saloon. His eyes had been the color of polished slate then, and as cold as ice. Now, with Benjamin in his arms, those same eyes were warm, and the same blue as a cloudless summer sky.

Sighing, Rebecca finished the last of her coffee and stood up. The dirty dishes spread out before her on the table seemed to have increased in number. She stretched, both hands at the small of her back as she fought fatigue.

"Can I help?" the driver said, nodding at the table.

At first Rebecca appeared to take him seriously. She

was, in fact, almost hopeful that he was sincere. But too many years of living with Josiah among the Prophets of Solomon had convinced her otherwise. *Women's work*, she reminded herself. "It's all right, Mr. Tyree," she smiled. "I just can't decide what I want to do first, bathe the baby or do the dishes!"

Tyree looked at the litter that covered the table, his eyes drifting from one place setting to the other. "I'll give the boy a bath," he said finally. Anything, he reckoned, was better than doing a mess of dishes.

Unable to help herself, Rebecca laughed. "I'm sorry," she apologized. "It's just that I have a difficult time picturing you doing anything remotely connected with taking care of a baby!"

Tyree's gray eyes warmed. The woman's words were as much of a dare as the ones Billy Starbuck had written for the paper. "Just watch me," he said.

He handed the woman the baby and went to the sink. There was a large, oval pan in the cabinet underneath, filled with spider webs and grimy from disuse. Tyree gave it a quick scouring. Then he disappeared outside, just long enough to pack the pan to overflowing with clean snow. He tucked it under his arm and carried it back inside. The cold enamel popped and hissed as he put the basin on top of the wood-burning cookstove. "When it's ready," he teased, "I'll just toss the boy in and boil him until he's done!" He reached out, taking the child and holding him close.

Rebecca was shaking her head in mock disapproval. She ladled out some water from the steaming pot on the stove and poured it over the snow in the basin. In minutes the water and snow combined to blend into a tepid, soothing pool.

Still holding Benjamin, Tyree used his free hand to clear a spot at the end of the long table, making room for the basin. He began undressing the little boy.

Rebecca reached out and rolled up Tyree's shirt sleeves. The skin on his arms was shockingly white compared to the darker skin of his hands, which still bore a hint of last summer's tan. "Are you sure you want to do this?" she asked, smiling.

Tyree nodded. "Just get the soap."

A warmth filled the room, something more than the rise in temperature caused by the moist heat from the baby's tub and Rebecca's full dishpan.

Tyree surrendered to a feeling of intimacy caused by the domestic tasks he and Rebecca were performing. He concentrated on the baby, gently washing the small fingers and toes, laughing as the little boy bent forward to blow bubbles against the bar of white soap that floated on the surface of the water.

There was a tenderness in Tyree that belied his usual gruff demeanor. Rebecca finished the dishes and turned from the sink, watching as he purposely prolonged the bath, which could have been accomplished in minutes. She hated to stop him, but for the baby's sake, she knew that she must. "He'll get cold, Simon," she chided softly, not realizing she had used his first name.

He nodded, taking the towel she offered him. He confidently lifted the infant from the water and, noticing the questioning look in Rebecca's eyes, said, "My son was about this old when I enlisted to fight in Mr. Lincoln's war."

Rebecca resisted the urge to help Tyree as he dried the little boy. She remained silent, waiting for him to continue, and when he didn't, she finally yielded to her own curiosity. "And . . . ?" she asked, prompting him to go on.

Tyree hadn't talked about it in a long time. In fact, he had never talked about it to anyone other than himself. "I was gone five years," he began. "When I came home, the boy was almost six. He had a brand new baby sister—and he called another man daddy."

Tyree's gaze was fixed on the child beneath his fingers. "Five years is a long time," he said softly, and even he was surprised that there was so little bitterness in his tone. For years, it had been like a wound festering somewhere just beneath the surface, a wound that caused him terrible pain.

"That's no excuse, Simon," the woman replied. Her anger was not simple righteousness: She genuinely believed in the sanctity of a lifelong commitment. And then she considered her own situation with Josiah. . . . She shook away the bitter thought. "She should have waited for you, Simon."

"Maybe," he said. It surprised him that she was so judgmental, and he tried to explain. "It was as much my fault as hers." He thought of his wife, of his life with her before the war, and it was like trying to recall a story that he had once read and could no longer remember.

"We had a farm," he began again. "She was alone, trying to run the place, to raise the boy. She needed help, and I wasn't there. My best friend was," he finished. Losing his friend had hurt him almost as much as losing his wife. But the biggest heartache had come from losing his son. He picked up the little boy from the table and hugged him.

Rebecca had brought out a clean change of clothes for the baby. She offered no resistance when Tyree took them, knowing that he needed to keep his hands, as well as his mind, busy.

The stage driver eased the long-sleeved cotton shirt over the infant's head. And then he reached for the diaper—just as the little boy heeded nature's call.

The sudden, warm shower roused both the man and the woman from their separate reflections, and they scrambled to block the flow. Tyree laughed, good-naturedly, Rebecca joining in. With one hand, he held the clean diaper in place like a blotter until the baby was finished. "I should have remembered!" he remarked.

Rebecca handed him a dry diaper. "I should have reminded you," she said gently. Their fingers met briefly, and this time she did not pull away.

Billy Starbuck remained mounted. He was on a ledge, high above Clear Creek Station, well hidden by the darkness and the thick lower branches of the snow-laden evergreens.

He had been watching the way station since sunset, noting the comings and goings. He had seen both Josiah and Kyle Lassiter as they made their separate trips to the privy, just as he had seen Simon Tyree toting firewood and water. He remembered the driver doing a similar task at Tanner's store and grinned. "You better watch it, Simon," he said aloud, as if the man were there. "You hang around Rebecca much longer, she just might get you trained!"

Restless, the little black mare pawed at the snow. Starbuck held her in place. He still had things to do, but he had come here hoping that he would somehow catch another glimpse of Elizabeth. And then, one by one, he saw the lights inside the cabin go out, until only a solitary dim glow remained.

Tyree, he thought, *trying to figure out what happened to his soldier boys from Camp Sunset.* The thought evoked both laughter and a renewed sense of purpose. Resolute, Starbuck turned the mare away from the cabin and pointed her nose northeast.

Chapter Six

Simon Tyree could not sleep. He sat at the table, his head resting on his folded arms, his edginess refusing to subside. Around him, he heard the muted snoring and breathing of the others and cursed himself for not being able to join them.

He stood up, stretching, and went to the stove for another cup of coffee. Rebecca had refilled the pot before retiring with the baby to the small bedroom being used by her family. He had asked her to make the brew extra strong, and she had not disappointed him.

Coffee nerves tormented Tyree now as much as the gnawing feeling that everything had gone wrong. And then he heard the sound, his whole body responding as he felt an intense stab of extreme, unreasonable terror.

The noise came subtly, like a roll of distant spring thunder, and was almost imperceivable inside the cabin. Tyree stood in the middle of the room, the coffeepot still in his hand, slowly turning as he cocked an ear in an attempt to fix the direction. *Northeast*, he reckoned.

He swore. "Damn! *Goddamn!*"

Lassiter had also heard the sound. He emerged from the back room, bleary-eyed, his hair tousled and his clothes askew. "Dynamite," he breathed. Close on his heels came Owen Parsons.

"Starbuck," Tyree answered. He turned to Parsons.

"Exactly what did that message from the military say, about why they weren't here?"

Parsons picked up a cup and gestured for Tyree to pour him some coffee. "There was a wire from Captain Grant at Camp Sunset. 'An unexpected delay.' He said they'd be here the same time tomorrow."

Tyree nodded his head, his mind working feverishly. He retreated to the corner of the room where Parsons's battered desk sat, his fingers groping for the telegraph key. He tapped out a curt message, angrily shushing both Lassiter and Parsons. Grim-faced, he tried again. "It's dead," he reported.

Parsons, refusing to believe him, brushed the stage driver's hand away. "You send like you've got lead in your fingers, Tyree." His own fingers seemed to dance on the black-ebony button. "Man's touch is like his signature, or his voice," he growled. "The man on the other end doesn't recognize you, he ain't going to answer. Leastwise, not this time of night."

There was no response. Twice more Parsons tried, his last message aimed at the night man in Holbrook. There was no courtesy in Parsons's final assault on the key: Tyree distinctly made out the dot-and-dash spelling of the words "ignorant bastard" and a few more graphic phrases before the old man gave up.

"You think he cut the wire?" Lassiter asked.

"At least between here and Holbrook. And Camp Sunset." Tyree tugged at Parsons's arm. "Try Flagstaff," he ordered.

Parsons did as he was told. He tapped out his query, a smile coming as the first words of a reply were transmitted back, and then, midword, the wire went dead.

"Signal Ridge," Tyree breathed. The hill was northeast of Clear Creek, high above the main road leading from Holbrook, and was topped by a three-way junction of wire that carried all the transmissions north, east, and west. They had passed under the ridge on the way in.

The three men were surprised when Parsons's dead key came alive. The message came slowly, a long pause

between each word. Parsons said each one aloud: "I'll
. . . be . . . waiting . . . Starbuck." He shook his head in
amazement. "The cocky little bastard!" He knew without
trying that his key was once again dead.

"And now, Simon?" Lassiter asked.

Simon Tyree's head ached. It wasn't too hard now to
figure out what Billy Starbuck had done. Not only had he
cut wires on Signal Hill, he had in all likelihood used the
dynamite to block the roadway below so that the stagecoach could not turn back and the military could not
follow. Tyree gave himself a long moment to collect his
thoughts and then spoke softly, struggling to contain the
anger that was clawing at his belly. "He'll be waiting for us
at Devil's Canyon," he announced, "just like he promised."

Lassiter cast an angry look toward the bedroom where
the Simpsons still slept. "And what the hell do you figure
on doing?"

"Making the run. Just like we planned," Tyree answered, and then he smiled. "We haven't got anyplace
else to go but forward, Kyle. You heard the blast; you
know what he's done."

Lassiter shook his head. "We could stay put and let
him come to us."

"He won't do it, Kyle. He doesn't have to do it. We'd
have to leave this cabin eventually, for food, water, and
firewood. All he'd have to do is sit out there and pick us
off, one by one. But he doesn't want *us*. If what he wrote
in his letter to the paper is true, all he wants is to prove
he can take that gold off the coach, somewhere between
Devil's Canyon and Flagstaff."

Lassiter swore. "And you're going to let him."

"Not hardly," Tyree answered harshly and then was
silent. He waited until Parsons left for a trip to the outhouse and then spoke again. His eyes were on the strongbox that they had carried inside when they first arrived. It
rested against the far wall, looking somehow insignificant.
"I'm going to need some help, Kyle."

The guard snorted derisively. "Doing what?"

Tyree stared at the door to the back room, listening

for sounds that would tell him the others had wakened.
There was nothing but the sound of regular, muted breathing. "We're going to empty that box and stash that
payroll—as soon as we talk Parsons into going back to
bed." He knew better than to include the old man in his
plans. Twenty-five thousand dollars in gold might prove
too much of a temptation for a man who had been dirt
poor all his life.

Interested, Lassiter considered the driver's words,
then said, "And in the morning, Starbuck will see us
loading up . . ."

"Just like always," Tyree finished. "He'll never know
the difference."

Lassiter knew Tyree was right. This was as close as he
would ever come to getting Billy Starbuck. *To killing Billy
Starbuck*. "All right," he agreed.

They had a cup of spiked coffee waiting for Parsons
when he came back from the privy—one-fourth java, three-
fourths pure rotgut, and a generous dose of sugar. It took
two more cups before the stationmaster was ready to turn
in, but when he went, he went quietly, a foolish smile
pasted across his face. "But the team, Simon," the old
man argued. "Hell, only a couple of hours 'til you want me
to hitch up. Plumb foolish to go to bed now!"

"We'll take care of the team, Owen," Tyree cajoled.
Together, he and Lassiter steered the man toward the
bunk room and poured him into his bed.

Tyree and Lassiter inspected the front room for a
place to stash the gold. The sturdiness of the building both
impressed and frustrated them. There was not a loose
board in the floor or an uncemented stone in the hearth,
and any attempt to alter them would leave too obvious a
mark. Parsons would notice anything that was out of place
or any fresh scarring that appeared on the scorched stone
and worn floors.

Time was of the essence. The first light of dawn was
beginning to filter through the single, smoke-stained window, and Tyree could hear the stirrings and early morning
coughs of the others as they slowly came awake. "Here!"

he said finally, standing at the rear wall of the cabin, and he wondered why he hadn't thought of it before.

An old potbellied stove stood beside the back door, the black pipe haphazardly pulled away from the soot-encrusted chimney plate. One leg was missing, and the stove tilted sideways at a precarious angle. "Inside?" Lassiter whispered hoarsely.

Tyree shook his head. He tried the door in the front of the stove and found that it was rusted shut. "Inside the pipe," he answered, mentally measuring the space. It would be a tight fit, but he was sure they would make it.

They worked fast. Lassiter laughed, relishing the feel of the small sacks of gold coins and currency in his palms. "Mighty tempting, Simon. What's to say I won't come back after it without you?"

Tyree snorted. "You're too much like me, Kyle. You want Starbuck a hell of a lot more than you want the gold."

It was true, but Lassiter still considered it a temptation. "Maybe I'll have it all," he retorted.

"If we don't get Starbuck on the other side of the canyon, this is all we'll have left for bait, Kyle. You better think about that." Finished, he stood the pipe back upright and covered up all the traces of his handiwork. "We miss him and he finds out that box is empty, this is the first place he'll come looking."

Lassiter wiped his grimy hands on his pants. "Just a thought, Simon."

"Yeah," the driver answered. He knew he didn't have to worry. Lassiter had been on the right side of the law too long to change now. He could hunt and kill the thief who had maimed him, but he would not steal.

Tyree turned away from Lassiter and went directly to the cookstove. There was just enough water for another pot of coffee and a quick splash bath. He put the coffee on before he washed. There would be little enough time for breakfast.

*   *   *

One hour later, Simon Tyree held the door open for Rebecca Simpson, watching as she passed in front of him. The sweet scent of her cologne reached out to him, and he wondered if she, as much as Billy Starbuck, was responsible for his long, sleepless night. He barely acknowledged her greeting, choosing instead to pat the little boy's cheek.

"Simon?" Rebecca looked up into a face that fatigue had rendered almost unrecognizable. "Didn't you sleep at all?" she asked, genuinely concerned.

"Sure," he snapped. "All of ten minutes." Without another word, he helped her and the child up into the coach. Josiah and Elizabeth followed.

Lassiter was already up in the box. He reached out, giving Tyree a hand up. "You were right," he said.

Tyree was in no mood for guessing games. "About what?" he asked, separating the leather reins and then relacing them between his fingers.

"About the weather." Lassiter pointed to the roof of the way station. A large slab of melting snow and ice slipped from the cedar shingles and dropped to the ground in front of the door, water rushing down in its wake.

Tyree swore. He uncoiled the long snake whip and cracked it loudly above the front two horses' heads. His shrill whistle competed with the sound, and the coach lurched forward as the four horses leapt against the traces. They were in a full run by the time they reached the end of the clearing.

Billy Starbuck had returned to the ledge above the way station. He stayed only long enough to watch Tyree and Lassiter hitch up the team and load the strongbox, and then he took his leave.

Skirting the clearing well beyond the station, he rode the deer trails, heading for Devil's Canyon Station, the stage's next stop, kicking the mare into a run. He had fifteen miles to cover, and he would do it in a third of the time it took the stage.

The way station in Devil's Canyon was by far the most elegant and well-fitted establishment along the

Holbrook-to-Flagstaff run. Purchased outright from the stage line when the railroad was completed, the place had been converted into a lodge that during the summer months catered to easterners and titled Europeans looking for the fabled excitement and big game of the wild West.

Navaho Stage Line had entered into a temporary agreement with the new owners. In exchange for the use of the facility—the main building and the stock pens—the line agreed to provide a wintertime caretaker. The man was a jack-of-all-trades who acted as hostler for the stages running between Holbrook and Flagstaff and as handyman for the building, repairing the wear and tear caused by the ravages of the long, bitter winters. It was a lonely job, made worse by the way station's location. It sat not far from the eastern bank of Devil's Canyon Creek, a fairly wide tributary of the Little Colorado, and was surrounded on both sides by high cliffs at the entrance to the rugged hell of Devil's Canyon.

When Billy Starbuck arrived there, well before the stage, he scouted the outbuildings, looking for some sign of the caretaker.

His original plan had been changed the moment he realized that Elizabeth was on Tyree's stage. His first scheme had been simply to waylay the coach just after it crossed the small river, taking the strongbox and then disappearing into the maze that was Devil's Canyon, as he had done before. But this was no longer feasible. Now he needed horses—one for Elizabeth and a second to carry her belongings and the supplies they would need for the baby, in the event that their stay at his hideout turned into a long one.

The young outlaw realized that he was going to have to make sure that Tyree and Lassiter could not follow him. And that meant stopping the coach before it made the river crossing. *Before the new team had been hitched*, he realized, thinking of his own need for fresh horses.

Billy Starbuck, he mused, *famed outlaw of the West, is going to have to lower himself to the level of a common horse thief*. The thought repulsed him, but not so much that he changed his mind.

A door opened in the way station and then slammed shut. The noise roused Starbuck from his dismal daydream, and he watched as the lone hostler made his way to the outhouse, a mail-order catalog tucked under his arm. He was already unbuckling his belt as he disappeared inside.

Starbuck dismounted and quickly led his horse down into the clearing. He was grinning, boyishly thinking of the alternatives that were open to him as he approached the outhouse. It would be so easy: tipping over the privy so that it landed with the front opening against the ground. The impact would throw its occupant face forward, compacting him between the door and the seat in a rather awkward position, leaving him totally immobilized.

The temptation proved more than the young man could bear. He secured his horse's lead reins to a large rock and silently sprinted around the little building, his eyes searching for a suitable tool. A neat stack of fence poles next to the stock corral caught his gaze, and he eased one down from the top of the pile. There was a large rock at the rear of the privy, and the outlaw made use of it. Quickly jamming the seasoned fence pole beneath the four by four that formed the base of the outhouse, he used the small boulder as an effective fulcrum. When he applied the full force of his weight to his fence-post lever, the privy tipped precariously forward.

The hostler, Heinrich Mueller—tenor and former understudy with the Munich Opera, now part-time horse wrangler for Navaho Stage Line—cried out in surprise at the first leeward shift. As the privy crashed to the ground his voice rose in a stream of German and English curses that ended in an abrupt high C.

Billy Starbuck, from his vantage place behind the outhouse, saw a flash of white flesh and the soles of Mueller's boots. He congratulated himself on a job well done. It would take considerable time for the hostler to regain his freedom and his dignity.

Turning away from the open privy hole in the ground in front of him, Starbuck headed for the main corral. Four large bays paced in a nervous circle, stirred up by the noise and the swearing, chasing each other and shying away as the young man ducked between the rails.

Starbuck would need two of the animals, and the other pair he would chase away, so that none of the stage line's crew or passengers would be able to use them.

He used no lariat. With his voice, he soothed the animals, cajoling them into a corner. They pressed nervously against each other, staying in place as Starbuck approached. Reaching out, he caught hold of the rope halter on first one and then another. He led the two animals, one on either side, to the gate. There was a length of rope hanging from a fence post, and with it he tied the two horses together and then hitched the rope to the fence.

Starbuck kicked the pole railings loose from the gateposts, and then he went back to the corner of the pen where the two loose coach horses still cowered. The air was growing warm, and the two animals worked up a sweat as they resisted his attempts to get them through the gates without their teammates. He stopped for a moment, contemplated the horses' stubbornness, and then removed his mackinaw as he waved his arms wildly. The combined motion of the young outlaw's arms and the flutter of the coat as he removed it spooked the horses. They broke into a run, and Starbuck used the coat to guide them out of the pen. He watched as they disappeared into the bush, running as if they were tied together by an invisible string.

The two animals Starbuck had tethered at the gate called out and tried to follow, and it took the young man considerable time to calm them. Once they were subdued, he scratched the ears of the horse nearest him and said, "Now my pretties, to find you a suitable place to hide while we wait for our lady!" Inspired, he thought of the wide front doors of the station's main building, and he smiled.

It took him two trips. On the first, he led his own mare into the big front room. Next he guided the two coach animals. And then he sat down to wait.

Tyree kept the four horses at a full run. The rising sun and the warm, southerly winds ate away at the snow and ice, reducing the white ground cover to a gray slush and the roadbed to a swamp of chocolate-colored mud. It was tough going for the animals, whose winter-thick, dark coats were flecked with white foam at their necks and flanks.

The roadway began to narrow as the coach headed north into the long, wide funnel that formed the mouth of Devil's Canyon. A series of arroyos—gullies carved by the mountain runoff from hard rains or melting snows—ran parallel to the roadway on both sides, their high walls seeming to run off to infinity.

Tyree hated this stretch of road. It brought back vivid memories of the mountain passes in the old South, passes where so many of his comrades in the Civil War had fallen prey to Rebel bushwhackers. It made the hair on the back of his neck crawl, and nothing he could do or think dispelled the sensation.

He breathed a bit easier as the stage swung around the final curve and began the slight downward slope leading to the way station at the river's edge. Pulling back on the reins, he slowed the horses, his foot pressed hard against the brake as he eased them into a gentle lope.

The way station loomed before them, a comforting plume of blue-gray smoke spiraling up from the chimney. "Coffee," Tyree said aloud, hoping the stationmaster would have some ready when they arrived. He felt as though he had gone without sleep for a week.

"Strong coffee," Lassiter said, echoing his thought. He shifted in his seat, rolling his shoulders to ease the ache.

Tyree's eyes were busy. The feeling of vulnerability that had been with him back in the pass had returned. His foot slipped off the brake, and the stage lurched forward as he relaxed his hold on the leather ribbons. The coach picked up speed, and he did nothing more to slow the team.

"What are you doing?" Lassiter asked, his gaze locked firmly on the driver's face.

"Something's wrong," Tyree answered. He saw the empty corral, but that didn't disturb him as much as the tracks leading from the pen. *They're wrong*, he thought to himself, reading the jumbled signs in the melting snow. Some led off into the brush at the river's edge, and others led straight to the cabin's front door. Neither was right, Tyree thought. It was then that he saw the overturned outhouse.

Using the lash, he stood up in the driver's box, yelling out to the tired, confused horses as he urged them back into a full run. From within the coach he heard a confused outcry and looked back just long enough to see Josiah Simpson hanging half in and half out the door. "Get inside!" he roared, using the whip again.

Lassiter held on for dear life as the coach swayed away from the station's front door and careened back out onto the stage road. "Jesus Christ!" he screamed as he braced himself with his single arm.

"It's Starbuck!" Tyree shouted. "He's inside the station!"

Lassiter turned around in the box. He raised the shotgun, cursing as the barrel got hung up on the metal railing behind the seat. A flash of black appeared in the doorway of the station as Billy Starbuck, astride his mare, exploded through the opening. The two coach horses he had stolen trailed along behind.

Kyle Lassiter felt the intense frustration of drawing a bead on his target only to know that the man was too far away. He swore again, throwing down the shotgun, struggling to pull Tyree's rifle from the boot. He jammed the weapon against his side, levered a shell into the chamber, and fired. The shot went wild, the bullet plowing into the dirt well to the right front foot of the outlaw's black mare.

Billy Starbuck stared after the stagecoach. He saw Josiah dangling from its interior, his body stretched to the limits as the door flung wide against the side of the Concord and pulled him off his feet. Two sets of hands clutched at his legs and his upper torso, and for a long, breathtaking minute it appeared that they would fail to drag him back into the safe interior of the coach. And then the coach lurched and the door swung back, pushing the man inward and then slamming shut.

Starbuck glanced up, his gaze settling on the driver's box. He saw Tyree standing tall and powerful, his whip hand arched as he artfully applied the noisy lash. And then the outlaw spotted Lassiter.

The guard was kneeling on the seat, facing the rear, his right arm invisible but marked by the gleam of sun on metal. A second flash of light appeared in front of the guard's face, but this one was accompanied by a blue-gray puff of smoke. Starbuck saw the bullet hit the dirt at his feet before he ever heard the sound.

The mare he was riding screamed and reared straight up, almost toppling over, and Starbuck clawed at the animal's long mane in an effort to keep his seat. The horses trailing behind him reared up, too, tangling in the lead rope that was looped around the mare's saddle horn in front of Starbuck. The backward jerk pulled the rope across the outlaw's thigh with such force that the friction caused the fabric to smoke; the cloth burned away and a great red welt rose on his leg.

Starbuck didn't feel the pain until it was over. "Son of a bitch!" he whined. It was as if his leg had been cauterized with a red-hot blade.

Starbuck dropped backward over the mare's smooth rump, untangling the rope as he moved. He could not risk losing the horses, no matter how much of a difficulty they became, yet he did not want to remain in the saddle, in full view of the vengeful Lassiter, to once again become tangled in the ropes. He kept the horses bunched, staying well behind them as he crouched down. While he peered cautiously above the horses' backs, he watched the coach disappear from sight around a bend in the road that led to the river.

The outlaw at last felt safe. He took a deep breath, collecting himself as he peered out from between the milling horses. But his troubles weren't over.

There was a mighty roar from behind him, a rich, full voice lifting to curse him in two languages. Starbuck spun around just in time to see a disheveled Heinrich Mueller coming at him with a three-tined pitchfork.

Starbuck cast a quick look in the direction of the departed coach. Somehow, Kyle Lassiter's rifle seemed less menacing than the German and his pitchfork. In true dime-novel tradition, Billy Starbuck vaulted up and over the black mare's rump, directly into his saddle, and rode off toward the river, leaving the irate stationmaster waving his pitchfork and cursing.

Chapter Seven

Simon Tyree slowed the stage team as they neared the wide river. A layer of inch-deep water shimmered atop the gray ice, but the surface seemed solid enough. Tyree snapped his whip, and the four big horses began to cross.

The Concord was already halfway across by the time Billy Starbuck rode around the bend into sight. Tyree had no choice but to keep the team at a slow walk. The horses danced nervously, unsure of their footing, the fragile ice made more treacherous by the thin layer of water.

Kyle Lassiter saw Starbuck come into view. Turning away from the riverbank, he whispered, "Hold the coach steady." Then he dropped down to the floor of the driver's boot as he slowly cocked the rifle. Seeing Tyree's questioning expression, he said, "I don't want him to see what I'm doing until I turn around."

Tyree nodded and pulled the horses to a halt. Kneeling in the box next to him, Lassiter closed his eyes for a brief moment. His entire countenance changed, his body compacting like a spring in a trap as he mentally prepared himself. Finally ready, he slid up onto the seat and took aim.

The only thing he saw was an empty stage road. Billy Starbuck was gone.

Kyle Lassiter swore, the anger welling up from deep

inside him as he shouted obscenities into the stillness behind the coach. "Bastard!" he screamed. The word echoed throughout the length of the canyon, mocking him.

When Billy Starbuck had started toward the frozen river, he had realized at once that he would be a sitting duck in Lassiter's sights if he tried to cross with three horses that would slide and prance while trying to run in three different directions at the same time. He spun his horse around and rode partway up the road. Then he abruptly turned and led the horses into the trees, heading downstream toward a narrow ford near his secret haven within Devil's Canyon.

Starbuck managed to keep the horses at a near run as they wound their way through the trees. He had traversed this area many times in the past and knew each twist and turn, each low-hanging branch and outcropping of rock. He rode on now, pacing himself as he moved downstream toward a narrow stretch of river. The water that covered the ice in this place seemed deeper than at the crossing back at the station, but the mare had made this crossing many times, swimming the narrow gap in the late autumn as easily as she now trotted across the winter ice.

Starbuck patted the mare's neck as they moved up the other bank of the river onto dry land. Then he turned to check the spare mounts. They followed him easily now, accepting his mare as their leader and matching her gait. Starbuck urged her into a trot and then into a ground-eating lope, secure in the knowledge that he would be waiting when the coach reached the opposite shore. He could barely wait to see the look on Elizabeth's face when she first saw him.

When he rescued her and freed her from Josiah.

Lassiter was angry. He reached out, trying to take the reins from Tyree's hands. "For Christ's sake, Simon! We're sitting ducks out here in the middle of the river, ripe for the taking. Get on with it!"

Roughly, Simon Tyree pushed the man's hand away. "Listen!" he ordered. "Shut up and listen!"

The ensuing quiet was almost terrifying. For a time, there was nothing but the occasional wisp of a horse's tail and the soft ring of harness metal as the team backed up in its traces. But then, suddenly, all four horses' heads came up, their nostrils flaring as they sensed something beyond the hearing of the men. They stood in place, quivering, their feet seeming to be solidly embedded in the ice just below the surface of the water.

Tyree stared down at those feet. Knowing it didn't matter, he surrendered the reins to Lassiter. "They won't move, Kyle," he said. "Not now." Without saying anything more, he dropped down over the side, pausing for a moment with one foot on the hub of the front wheel, the other just inches above the rising water.

"Tyree?" Josiah Simpson called from inside the coach. When the driver didn't answer, Josiah opened the door. He, too, remained where he was, his gaze locked on the water beneath him.

Tyree dropped down onto the ice. "You know what's happening?" he asked softly, not wanting to alarm the women.

Josiah nodded. He ducked back inside the Concord, his voice betraying nothing as he spoke to his wives. And then he reappeared. He disembarked from the coach, careful to shut the door behind him. He had already pulled down the leather shades. "Moving water," he said when he joined Tyree beside the front wheel. A small twig floated serenely between them, moving downstream with the current.

Simon Tyree nodded. With Josiah carefully following him, he moved forward, stopping when he was even with the rear end of the horse nearest the coach. He placed a reassuring hand on the animal's rump and stared off into the northwest, toward Flagstaff. The San Francisco Mountains loomed on the distant horizon, twelve thousand feet above sea level, the majestic peaks hidden in the silver clouds. *Rain clouds*, Tyree observed grimly. He shook his head.

Josiah Simpson spoke aloud what Tyree was thinking. "False spring," he observed.

Tyree nodded. The horse he was petting tensed beneath his fingers, and he watched as the animal's legs went rigid. It was as if the gelding were bracing himself in expectation of something that only he could sense.

There was a grinding sound, a noise that was felt more than heard, as the ice beneath Tyree's feet vibrated. The sensation lasted only a moment, and then it was quiet again. "It's breaking up," Tyree murmured.

"Jesus," Josiah Simpson breathed. It was more a profane oath than a whispered prayer, and he mumbled a quick apology.

"Get back in the coach," Tyree ordered.

"Are we going to make it?" Josiah asked. There was no fear in his voice. He simply wanted to know.

"I don't know," Tyree answered truthfully. For the first time, he looked at the man. "You should be with the women," he said. When he realized that Josiah misunderstood his meaning, he raised his hand. "If you stay out here, they'll know something is wrong."

Josiah's smile was sardonic. He felt the ice beneath his feet tremble a second time. "Well," he breathed, "something is." He turned and went back to the coach.

Tyree remained where he was. He stared at his own feet for a time, watching as the flow increased in speed and the water crept up his boots in small but measurable degrees. The speed of the debris that passed his feet had increased as well. "I'm going to try walking the horses, Kyle," he called up to the man sitting in the box.

Lassiter nodded. He didn't envy Tyree's position. They couldn't turn back now since they were closer to the opposite shore than to the station at their backs, and it was far too dangerous to attempt walking off the river across the unstable ice. By far the safest place was in the Concord. If the water continued to rise, the well-constructed coach would float on top of it like a barge. But alone on the ice, Tyree was every bit as vulnerable as the horses.

Tyree moved to the head of the team. He ducked under the lead horse's neck, placing himself between it and its teammate. A bridle strap in each hand, he clucked softly to the animals and then took a single step forward.

The matched bays hesitated but then followed after the driver, lifting their front feet high above the water and pawing at the air before each step. In their earlier panic, the horses had backed up in their traces, and it took several cautious steps before the slack was taken up and the coach began to move.

The heavy, ironbound wheels remained motionless for a time and then wrenched free, concave indentations cut into the ice as they rolled forward. An irritating *cr-r-un-ch* sounded from all four wheels, and it continued as they turned.

Tyree heard the sound, his mouth going dry as he realized what was happening. The sun-warmed water that was rapidly flowing across the face of the ice was eating away at the frozen mass, softening it, and the weight of the coach was causing the wheels to sink deeper and deeper. It was only a matter of time, Tyree thought, until . . .

The thing he feared most happened. The left forward wheel of the Concord suddenly dropped through the ice. The coach jerked to a stop, tilting at such a sharp angle that Lassiter was almost thrown from the seat. Using his feet, the man braced himself, quickly knotting the reins around the brake to free his hand so he could hold on.

Tyree's arms were almost torn from the sockets as the two horses he was leading stopped dead and tossed their heads. There was a moment of silence and then almost a sigh as the right front wheel broke through the ice to rest on its wide hub.

Tyree let go of the horses. He held his breath as he moved, one slow step at a time, back toward the coach.

"Simpson," he called. He shook his head when Lassiter offered to come down. "I need two more hands, Kyle.

And I need you up there, watching for Starbuck." He was telling the truth, not trying to assuage the man's ego.

Josiah cautiously stepped down from the passenger compartment and moved to Tyree. Anticipating the driver's question, he said, "Everyone's all right." Briefly, he averted his eyes. "Rebecca has things well in hand." He didn't need to say more: Elizabeth's whining voice carried loud and shrill on the air. She was crying.

"I need to unhitch the team," Tyree said. "I'll need your help. We'll tie a rope to the coach, and I'll try to lead the horses to shore and secure the line. When the ice breaks up, I'll use the horses to pull the coach in. Understand?"

Josiah nodded, and the two men set about unhitching the rear pair of horses from the coach. They worked quickly yet carefully, concerned that they might startle the animals and make them spook. Together, they worked their way to the lead pair, unhooking the long set of reins, one man on each side as they coaxed the animals away from their restraints.

Stubbornly, the animals balked. The mare Josiah was leading suddenly reared up, carrying the man with her. She came down stiff-legged, stood level on the ice, and then broke through. Josiah went through the brittle ice beside her.

Tyree lunged across the floe in front of the horses, his hand closing around Josiah's collar. He held on to him, keeping him afloat, at the same time easing himself belly-down at the edge of the widening hole. The terrified struggling of the downed horse made matters worse: The animal's legs flayed wildly as the mare futilely attempted to swim. The swell of water that rose around her churned like a whirlpool, and Tyree could feel Josiah being pulled down and under, away from his grasp.

Josiah cried out as the mare's shod hoof collided with his leg. The pain seemed to fill him with a great surge of energy, and he wrapped both hands around Tyree's arm and pulled himself upward until he could get his knees up against the horse. And then he let go of Tyree, using the harness on the mare to pull himself up out of the water. He clambered across her back, belly-flopping onto the ice at Tyree's side, where he lay, his head at Tyree's feet, breathing hard, slowly regaining his strength until he was able to rise up and stand.

While Josiah recovered, Tyree rose to his feet beside the gaping hole. He looked at the panic-stricken mare as she struggled in the water, the heavy harness weighing her down. He realized at once that, surrounded by ice, the animal had no chance of escape.

"Kyle!" Tyree shouted. He lifted his arm, gesturing to the guard. At the sound of his voice, the mare stopped struggling. She looked up at him, stretching out her neck and laying her head on the ice at his feet. The water on top of the ice was sucked into her lungs as she inhaled, and her brown eyes widened. The dark orbs were soon ringed with white, panic taking her again, and once more she wildly began treading water.

Lassiter stood up. He tossed the rifle to Tyree, who caught it just as the second lead horse broke through the ice beside the mare.

Tyree swore, truly grieved by what he had to do. He cocked the rifle, aimed, and fired. Once. Twice. The bodies of the two horses were sucked under by the current and disappeared under the ice.

"No-o-o-o!" a muffled voice screamed at Tyree from the shoreline, something remorseful and accusatory in the single word.

Lassiter thumbed back the hammers on the shotgun he still held and peered into the thick line of pines that rimmed the shore. He saw nothing.

Tyree propped the rifle across his shoulder. He faced his unseen judge on the shoreline and called out to him. "Starbuck!" There was no answer. He tried again. "Billy Starbuck!"

Josiah was beside Tyree now, both arms wrapped around his own body as he tried to get warm. He softly repeated the name Tyree had called. "Starbuck." It slowly dawned on him what was happening, what had been happening all along. "*He's* the reason you didn't want to take us to Flagstaff," he said, surprise making the statement sound like a question.

"We're carrying the railroad payroll," Tyree explained. "And he wants it."

Josiah's gaze swept the riverbank. "Enough to let us die?" he asked incredulously.

Tyree shrugged. "Maybe." His voice raised as he called out to the outlaw again. "I know you're there, Starbuck!" he roared. "And I know what you want!"

Still not visible to those on the ice, Starbuck finally called out to them, his voice clear but unrecognizable above the din of the rushing waters. "You're going to need some help to make it to shore, Tyree! What say we make a trade?"

The driver moved slightly, standing sidewise as he positioned himself in such a way as to be able to see the shoreline and Kyle Lassiter on the coach. "What kind of trade?" he shouted, playing the game.

Starbuck laughed. "The money, Tyree!" he answered. "Your money or your lives!"

Tyree's laughing reply was humorless. "Uh-huh," he said, as if thinking out loud. "I figure a way to send you the box, and then you help us off the ice. That about how *you've* got it figured, Starbuck?"

"Why not?" the outlaw answered. His arrogant reply revealed that he was confident he had the upper hand. "Seems fair to me."

The voice coming from the shoreline was menacing, but at the same time it was vaguely familiar, despite the loud rush of the river. Simon Tyree shook his head. The water at his feet was running faster and deeper. "Why don't you just give us a hand, Starbuck? Then we'll talk."

Tyree was puzzled by the outlaw's toying with them. Billy Starbuck had never killed anyone during a robbery— but that, Tyree now figured, was largely a matter of luck and circumstance. The young man had never really been pushed. Tyree looked up to see Lassiter caressing his

shotgun, uncomfortable in the realization that he was between the guard and his much-wanted prize. "Starbuck?"
he called.

"I want the box, Tyree," the outlaw answered.

The driver said nothing for a moment. "No," he said
finally. "If you don't help us, I'll keep the box. You can
swim for it!" He gave the outlaw some time to consider his
words. Behind him, the coach shifted again as the rear
wheels broke through, leaving the coach resting on its
chassis in the ice. The baby began to cry. "It's sinking,
Starbuck! The coach, the horses, my passengers—and the
strongbox."

Billy Starbuck considered the man's words, a sense of
panic beginning to claw at his belly. He wanted the money,
almost as much as he wanted Elizabeth. The problem was
to figure a way to get what he wanted without exposing
himself. Without getting himself killed.

"Get rid of the guns, Tyree!" the outlaw shouted.
"The guard's shotgun, and that rifle of yours." There was a
nervous edge to his voice as he made his demands, and
that uneasiness made him forget that Tyree also wore a
handgun—a revolver hidden beneath the bulk of his winter clothing. "I have two extra horses," he yelled, sweet-
ening the pot. "I can rig a towline!"

Tyree was running out of time, and he knew it.
"Kyle," he said softly, levering a cartridge into the chamber of the rifle.

"Go to hell, Simon," the guard answered.

Tyree brought the rifle up, until it was pointed directly at Lassiter. "I won't kill you, Kyle," he said quietly.
"I'll just put a slug through your good arm and let you
spend the rest of your life trying to figure out how to get
even." The cruelty was intentional: He wanted Lassiter to
know that he didn't have time to indulge the man's need
for revenge against Billy Starbuck. Holding the guard at
bay, he spoke to Josiah. "Get the shotgun, Simpson." The
last thing he wanted now was Lassiter dropping the cocked
weapon onto the ice.

"I'll take it, Mr. Tyree." Rebecca Simpson stepped

down from the coach. Lifting her skirt, she walked carefully across the ice until she was directly abreast of the driver's box. "I don't want to die, Mr. Lassiter," she said softly, looking up at him. "At least, not here, and not like this." She gestured at the ice-covered river, tilting her head as she listened for something that she knew the guard also heard. It was the distant roar of rushing water somewhere upstream, and it was growing louder. She held out her hand.

Lassiter surrendered the shotgun. He had witnessed a spring flood, years before, when he was a boy. The stink of mud and death had never left the dark corners of his mind.

Rebecca carried the gun to Tyree. She handed it to him as if it were an offering. "Please, Simon, get us out of here," she begged. She wasn't afraid for herself, but she was deathly afraid for the baby and the others.

Tyree nodded tersely and then said, "Now get back in the coach with the baby. It'll float. It's the safest place if the ice gives way completely."

As Rebecca complied, Tyree took Lassiter's shotgun and lifted it above his head. And then, along with his rifle, he dropped it into the same watery grave that had taken the two horses.

On the riverbank, Billy Starbuck moved out on horseback into the light. He paused at the water's edge just long enough to pull the silk neckerchief up over his nose. And then, cautiously, he urged his horse out onto the ice. He had already tied his long rope to a towering pine, and he reeled it out behind him as he moved.

Tyree called out to him when the mare balked. He pointed to the horse. "She senses a soft spot," he called. "Stay put and toss me the line!"

It took two tries before Tyree could latch on to the rope when Starbuck threw it. He had to venture out from the coach some twenty feet before he caught the end. There was only sixty feet of line, and when he did catch it, he realized it was too short to reach the coach.

Starbuck was torn by what was happening. There was

more rope back at the cabin, but there was no more time. Already, the water on top of the ice had reached the curved bottom of the big Concord.

Tyree looked up at Lassiter. "There's a rope under the driver's seat," he bellowed. "We'll run it through the front wheels and hitch the ends to the towline. That's the only way to extend the line so it'll reach the coach!"

Lassiter climbed down with the rope and handed it to Tyree, who looped the long cord through the exposed upper sections of the Concord's front wheels twice. Then he snaked the ends back along the ice and joined them to Starbuck's rope with a series of strong knots. When he was through, he called out to the man on the shore. "Make sure you've tied us off securely, Starbuck! You hear me?"

Starbuck rode back to the riverbank and checked the knots that held the rope to the ponderosa pine. Meanwhile, the ice continued to break up around the coach, until it was on little more than a frail island caught in place in a bottleneck of ice chunks in the middle of an increasingly fast-running current. Buffeted by the rising water, the shelf tilted, the weight of the coach and the horses threatening to tip it belly-up. Tyree moved to even the weight, grateful as Josiah and Lassiter each grabbed one of the two remaining horses and worked with him to steady the floe. At the river's edge, Billy Starbuck had dismounted and was working furiously to strengthen the knots that secured the line to the tree.

Elizabeth Simpson, an impatient curiosity getting the best of her, chose this moment to step out of the coach. She had left the baby behind with Rebecca in a wicker clothes basket made up as a traveling bed. Terror swept her as she found herself nearly knee-deep in icy water. Hysterically, she began to scream, a series of short, high-pitched shrieks that came with increasing frequency and ended in one long wail.

Josiah raced across the floe, upsetting the precarious balance that was needed to keep the frigid island steady. As he grabbed the young woman, the horse he had been holding at his side followed after him. Their weight, along with the weight of the panic-stricken young woman, combined to tip the ice at a steep angle, lifting the other edge entirely out of the water.

The panicked horse suddenly slid along the ice and plunged into the water. Before they could react, Josiah and Elizabeth went sliding after it and disappeared with the current. As the island of ice lurched back in the other direction, Lassiter and the remaining horse went plummeting off the other end into the river and were swept away through swift-running channels in the ice. Simon Tyree was thrown facedown upon the ice floe and barely escaped being carried off in the rush of water by grabbing hold of the front wheel.

As the remaining ice broke up and the water raged higher around the coach, Tyree slowly pulled himself up along the wheel. From inside the coach, Rebecca screamed, "Simon!" as she reached out the window and tried to grasp his arm. Realizing she could not reach him from so high, she opened the door, braced herself against the jamb, and leaned out.

The Concord was taking on water, the open door allowing the cold water to rush into the interior of the coach. Tyree managed to hook his foot on one of the spokes of the wheel, and as he stepped up, he grabbed hold of Rebecca's arm. With his other hand gripping the edge of the open window, he fought the growing current and pulled himself into the coach, slamming the door behind him.

A wall of water came down the canyon now, rolling toward the stagecoach like the tide of a great ocean. Smaller swells rushed before it, eating at the remaining ice that had imprisoned the wheels of the great old coach until it was torn away. The Concord righted itself and leveled out, and then it began to float, held in place against the current by the ice jam and by Billy Starbuck's rope.

As the ice jam broke up and the coach began to ride the current, Tyree looked out the window at the taut towline Starbuck had attached to the ponderosa pine. If the line held, it would serve to pull the coach to the riverbank as the current forced the vehicle downstream.

Tyree looked over at Rebecca, who had taken the little baby into her arms. He sat beside her and wrapped his arms around them both. "It will be all right," he soothed. "Everything will be all right."

As if mocking him in reply, the long towline screeched with the strain. The knots holding the two ropes together held, but the knots securing the line to the tree stretched and suddenly gave way with a snap as fierce as the popping of Tyree's bullwhip. Still caught in the midstream current, the stagecoach picked up speed as it careened downstream.

Tyree lay back against the seat, seized by a need to laugh and cry as he clung tightly to Rebecca and the baby. The coach bobbed up and down, as seaworthy as the tall ships that had given the Concord its nickname—"clipper ship of the desert."

Chapter Eight

Billy Starbuck raced along the shore, his lungs rebelling as he ran over the rough terrain. Ahead of him, in the water, he could see the struggling figures of Josiah and Elizabeth. They were being carried along by the current, buffeted and tossed among forest debris and chunks of ice that were filling the deepening and widening river.

The outlaw's boots were not made for running, and he cursed the vanity that had made him buy them. He paused for only a moment to pull them off, awkwardly hopping first on one foot and then the other until he was finally in his stocking feet and able, in spite of the cold and the pain, to run. He sprinted like a young deer, following the course of the water, slowly gaining ground in his race to catch up with his brother and Elizabeth.

Starbuck watched in horror as Elizabeth tumbled along the surface of the water, her dark skirt billowing out and then sinking into the river, the sheer weight of the heavy fabric beginning to pull her down.

The young man dove into the river. He was a strong swimmer, and he cut through the water, using the current to increase his speed. Elizabeth went down, once, then again. Her pale face reappeared doll-like above the water, as if she had lost her will to struggle. She was going down for a third time when he reached her, his arm closing around her waist. He drew her close. Oblivious of their peril and overcome by emotion, he kissed her.

When he resumed swimming, he did not fight the water. Again, he let the force of the current work for him. It carried him downstream, toward a familiar bend of the river. Starbuck knew that they would be all right, that soon *everything* would be all right.

Rebecca Simpson stared out the leeward window of the Concord. She was grateful to be alive, and even more thankful that Simon Tyree and the little boy had been spared. But the others . . .

A distant blur of color appeared in the water, and Rebecca recognized Josiah and Elizabeth. She saw the younger woman carried away from Josiah, just as the tall upper portion of a large pine smashed into Josiah's broad back. He disappeared beneath the water and was lost from view for a moment. Rebecca's gaze froze on the spot, and she watched as the big pine rolled over. The tree changed course, turning around, and Rebecca saw Josiah's still form among the thick, green branches. The treetop continued to spin around, faster and faster, caught by the whirlpool current of a river gone wild, until it was driven around the bend and out of sight.

Clutching the baby to her chest, Rebecca sank to her knees, a great sorrow tearing at her heart. If there truly was a hell, then it existed here, in this place, a part of the terror that filled this canyon.

Simon Tyree saw her face and knew what she was thinking. He reached out, touching her cheek, and wished that he could comfort her. Instead, he lifted the infant and took him in his arms. "We've got to keep him warm, Rebecca," he said softly as he wrapped another blanket from the basket around the child. Rebecca responded to his actions and sat back up. Brushing the wetness from her eyes, she took the baby in her lap and carefully bundled him in the blanket. Swept along by the current, the stagecoach continued down the river and followed Josiah around the bend. Suddenly there was a jarring crash, and the coach shuddered to a halt.

Tyree looked out the window and saw that they were caught halfway between midstream and the riverbank. "We must have hit a sandbar," he explained. He could hear the force of the current striking the rear of the vehicle. He stared at the interior of the coach, his eyes assessing the damage—the wetness. "We've got to get out of here."

Tyree's mind was busy. The mountain storm responsible for the flood had followed the river south, dissipating as it moved across the high plateaus. A gentle rain was falling now, a warm rain that pattered against the top of the coach with a deceptive rhythm belying its true power. And with the rain came a calmness, a serenity that made it easy to think.

Tyree rose up from his seat, his hand on the metal handle of the door. He opened it just a crack and leaned out. The river was wider here, and the flow of the current had eased. The yellow, silt-filled water was almost pacific now, the current less threatening than before. It was calm enough, he reasoned, to chance a swim to shore.

"Rebecca," he began, still staring out at the water, "I'm going to try to make it to shore."

She inhaled sharply. She was as afraid of being alone in the Concord as she was of Tyree getting hurt. But closing her eyes against the fear, she declared, "You'll make it, Simon." Her voice was surprisingly strong.

It was all the encouragement he had wanted. Keeping his back to her, he slowly began to disrobe, the heavy fur coat first, then his shirt and boots. He was careful to wrap the pistol in his shirt and place the bundle high on the seat back in the coach. Without looking back, he reached out to Rebecca and felt the reassuring warmth of her touch. "It's going to be all right," he promised.

Rebecca felt him slip away from her, his fingers seeming to linger and tighten just before he let go. She watched as he lowered himself into the water, sorry when he shut the door that she had encouraged him. She heard him push away from the body of the coach and then heard the slow, steady stroke of his arms cutting through the water.

Tyree made his way to the front of the coach and discovered that, as he had thought, the vehicle had struck a sandbar and was now sitting in water that was chest deep. Taking a deep breath, he dove underwater and began searching for what was left of the submerged towline by feel rather than sight. The line was well below the surface of the water, and he stayed under just long enough to grab hold of it and pull it up. Straining to keep one hand on the line, he swam toward shore.

He was thoroughly fatigued when he pulled himself up on the bank, and after securing the towline to a small tree, he sat for a time, his head between his knees, taking deep breaths and then coughing up the water he had swallowed. He soon began to feel the cold and knew he had to move.

A soft nicker greeted him as he rose to his feet. He turned, a wave of gratitude filling him as he saw the two horses Billy Starbuck had stolen from the Devil's Canyon station. They were ankle-deep in water and apparently had wandered down the riverbank, following the familiar stagecoach.

Tyree called out to the horses. He moved toward them, his hand extended, palm upward, sorry that he didn't have some treat for them. Neither horse cared: They welcomed the touch of the man's hand, taking comfort from his closeness.

"I need your help, Tyree."

The driver turned, startled at the sound of a human voice. He found himself staring at Billy Starbuck, then swore vehemently. "Son of a bitch! It's *you!*" he exploded. "*You!*" He raked the young man with his eyes and searched the near landscape for a stout club.

Billy Starbuck—young Will from the stage office—stood barefoot before Tyree, his dark, soaking whipcords pasted against his lean form. Elizabeth Simpson was in his arms, the weight of her body and her wet clothes almost more than he could carry. "I . . ." he began. "I . . ."

When the young man seemed to swoon and then fell to his knees, Tyree bolted forward and grabbed Elizabeth, sweeping her away as the outlaw fell forward onto his face. Starbuck lay still for several moments, breathing hard, then tried to rise up and could not, his arms numb. Then the feeling returned, to his fingers first and then to the long muscles in his forearms. A stabbing pain rippled through his biceps and shoulders, so excruciating that he almost passed out.

Tyree laid the woman down. He put his hand on Starbuck's back. "Take it slow," he cautioned. He began massaging the muscles of the young man's neck, working them like a baker kneading bread, asking himself why he wasn't strangling him instead. "Will," he snorted, "is Billy Starbuck. *Thief!*" he said contemptuously. That the younger man could have deceived him so thoroughly—so easily—riled him. He gave the young man's shoulders a final, hard squeeze.

Starbuck yelped. Tyree's ministrations were worse, now, than the cramps. He twisted away from the older man's fingers. "Man's got to make a living," he snapped, flexing his arms.

"You ever hear of work?" Tyree retorted. "Full-time, regular work for a regular wage?" He inhaled, calming himself. "We haven't got time for this," he said.

He turned his attention to Elizabeth, watching as Starbuck attempted to revive her. Shoving the younger man aside, he leaned down to listen to her heart. She was breathing, slow and regular. "She's going to be all right," he said, standing.

"But . . ." Starbuck also rose to his feet.

Tyree went back to the two coach horses. "She's got a pretty good knot on the back of her head, and she had the wind knocked out of her. But her lungs sound clear, and her heart's beating like a drum." He jabbed a finger at the outlaw. "We've got to get the coach in here," he said. He jerked his head at the setting sun. "It's going to get damned cold once that sun sets, and we're going to need cover. At least until we can figure a way out of here."

"Or until someone comes looking," the younger man said. He had no intention of telling Tyree about his cabin, not while he still had a chance to take the money.

"That's not likely," Tyree groused. If there had been flooding in Devil's Canyon, there had been more farther north and west. It would be a long while before anyone bothered to come looking for a lost stagecoach. "Give me a hand," he ordered.

"We going to tow her in?" Starbuck asked as he took hold of the two horses.

Tyree nodded. "The river's calmer down here. We'll use the towline to pull her in. But we'll have to rig a harness first."

"Harness," Starbuck murmured. "There's no harness."

"You always been that smart? Or is that something that you managed to figure out in the past five minutes?" Tyree asked. He grabbed the young man's arm. "I said we'd *rig* a harness."

Tyree's resourcefulness impressed the younger man. He watched as the driver fashioned a makeshift harness for the first horse from his own denim trousers. It was crude, similar to something the outlaw had seen in the schoolbooks Rebecca had used to instruct him in his youth—in the old woodcuts of English serfs who worked the king's land. A simple yoke around the animal's neck, one pantleg on either side, the seat of the man's trousers fitting across the horse's chest and down between the front legs. It would never work for a long haul, but it would be enough to steady and guide the coach.

"Well," Tyree grimaced, making his final knot, "that's number one."

It took a moment for the man's words to sink in. Billy Starbuck was suppressing a laugh, thinking of how ridiculous Tyree looked in his sagging, trap-door long johns, when suddenly it hit him. "No," he said, without thinking. "Hell, no!"

"Take 'em off," Tyree ordered. "Now."

Starbuck stared first at Tyree and then at the stagecoach in the middle of the river. Reluctantly, he unbuckled his belt and stepped out of his trousers.

Already, the sun had begun to drop behind the dark evergreens that studded the shoreline. A thin, gray vapor began to emanate from Tyree, the cold air robbing him of his warmth. He knew how desperate their situation was, and how much more danger they faced. He thought of Rebecca, and it made him work harder and faster.

He went into the water, making the long, cold swim back to the coach to make sure the lines were still tight and to tell Rebecca what they were doing, and then he returned to hitch up the team. "You ride," he shouted to Starbuck as he waded out into the river. He would stay in the water, making sure the line stayed free of tangling debris.

Having retrieved his boots and put them back on his feet, Starbuck located his mare and led her to where Tyree had revived him. He tied the mare's reins to a tree and then took the makeshift harness in hand and slowly urged the other two animals forward until the slack in the line was taken up. As the horses continued to pull, the coach behaved beautifully, rolling free of the sandbar and gliding with the current as it moved downstream to shore and finally landed.

Tyree opened the door. He reached up, taking Rebecca in his arms and gently lifting her out onto the ground. She buried her head against his shoulder and then turned to show him the baby. The little boy was sound asleep, snuggly wrapped in a single sleeve of Tyree's heavy jacket. "I knew you could do it, Simon," she smiled.

"Not by myself," he admitted. He half turned. "Billy Starbuck," he said, gesturing at the younger man, who was still mounted. He had turned the horses around and was heading straight for the coach.

Rebecca shaded her eyes against the setting sun and stared up at the man astride the wet horse. His features were indistinguishable for a time, the sun at his back, and it wasn't until he was only an arm's length away that

Rebecca recognized him. He slid from the horse's back and stood directly in front of her.

She looked up at him, her face alive with emotion, her eyes filled with a maternal warmth. And then she remembered Tyree's words: *Billy Starbuck*. "Oh, Will," she whispered to the outlaw. There was no censure in her tone, just concern and worry.

The young man looked at her, feeling enough shame for both of them and unable to meet her eyes. "Rebecca," he said softly.

She gathered him in her arms. It had been almost nine months since he had left the small, Solomonite settlement north of Holbrook.

Puzzled, Simon Tyree watched the reunion. It was obvious that the woman knew the young man, but the question of how and from where puzzled him. "Rebecca?" he questioned softly.

"He's Will Simpson—Josiah's brother," the woman answered when she let go. The mention of her husband's name brought back the reality of what had happened to all of them. "Josiah?" she murmured, her eyes searching the small clearing.

Tyree shook his head. "Will found Elizabeth," he said. "She's resting nearby. I don't know what happened to Josiah." He stared out at the water. "Or Lassiter," he finished. The instinct for his own survival—and for Rebecca's and the child's—had overshadowed his concern for the others.

Rebecca understood and said nothing, feeling her own guilt for not having asked about Josiah sooner. Her eyes swept the riverbank. "We have to look for them," she said. It was clear from her voice that she would not be dissuaded.

Tyree didn't want to argue with her, but neither would he give her any false hope. The question of their own deliverance still remained in doubt. "Later," he said softly. When the woman started to protest, he raised his hand. "After we've made camp and we have a fire. We must take care of the living, Rebecca."

She knew he was right, but it did not make the truth any easier. She turned to her brother-in-law. "Go get Elizabeth, Will, and bring her here," she said. "And Simon, you'll start the fire. And then you'll *both* find your pants."

Tyree looked down. He had completely forgotten about his trousers. "Oh, Jesus," he swore, embarrassed. The fact that Starbuck was laughing at him didn't help. "You heard what she said!" he shouted.

Starbuck quickly untied the makeshift harness. Standing well back, he offered Tyree the pants. Then he retrieved his own pants, put them on, and headed over to get Elizabeth.

Tyree put on the wet trousers, turning his back as he buttoned his fly. And then he marched off into the pines in search of firewood. He could feel Rebecca's amused gaze on his back and silently cursed her for her insolence.

Kyle Lassiter lay on his back in the mud. He was aware first of the growing cold and then of the heavy wetness of his clothes.

He knew nothing about how he had come to be cast ashore. His last memories were of the young woman, the terrible sound of her screaming, and the terrifying upheaval under his feet as the ice floe shifted and he was thrown into the water. Terror had possessed him then: the knowledge that he was in the river and had only one arm. He had thought that he was going to die—that perhaps he already *was* dead.

A dull pain in Lassiter's thigh brought back another memory. A coach horse had slipped into the water behind him, and he had desperately grabbed the animal's tail as it brushed his cheek. The horse's hind leg had nicked him more than once, he recalled, but after a while the pain didn't matter. All that mattered was that he was alive and that he would stay alive as long as he held on.

Lassiter turned his head. Without getting up, he stared at his surroundings, his eyes probing the terrain as he measured the length of the shadows and the position of the sun. He was on the west bank of the river, far down-stream of where he had gone into the water.

Far downstream of Billy Starbuck.

The thought warmed him, and he turned over on his knees. He was alive, and he considered his survival a sign from God: He was still alive to find and take Starbuck.

An eye for an eye, he thought, rubbing at the sore nub that hung from his left shoulder. *An arm for an arm.*

He had learned something when he was in the river, in that long moment of total emptiness when, he felt, he had departed this world. Death was simply an end, a black void where there was nothing: no pain, no fear, no eternal damnation.

There were things *worse* than death, he surmised. It was a lesson he intended teaching Billy Starbuck.

Chapter Nine

Elizabeth Simpson had regained consciousness. She sat at the riverbank, her knees drawn up to her belly, her teeth chattering. There was an angry pout on the young woman's face, a petulant frown that marred her otherwise attractive features. She was thinking of little else but her own suffering. And of Josiah.

It was his fault, she thought bitterly, all his fault. If it hadn't been for Josiah and his constant evangelizing, she would still be in the hotel in Holbrook—dry and with an abundance of hot food. She looked out at the desolate, mud-yellow river and hoped that the man was dead.

Her mind working with its usual efficiency, she thought of the things that had happened. She had purposely feigned unconsciousness when she was dragged from the river, unsure as to who had saved her. And she had remained that way, listening to the exchange between Simon Tyree and the outlaw, Billy Starbuck.

Starbuck. The name brought a smirk to Elizabeth's lips. She had almost cried out when she realized that the famous Billy Starbuck was none other than her brother-in-law, Will Simpson. *Will*, she mused. It was incredible: Her round-faced, groping brother-in-law, the young man she had toyed with out of boredom, had turned out to be Billy Starbuck.

"Beth?" The quiet voice called out to her, and there was something almost reverent in the tone.

Coyly, Elizabeth raised her head. Her lower lip trembled, and she began to cry. "Will?" she whispered tremulously. *"Will?"* Opening her arms, she reached out to him.

"Elizabeth," he murmured. Setting his rifle to one side, the young man dropped down to one knee and pulled the woman to his chest. An intense hunger touched him, and he kissed her. She seemed to melt in his arms, no innocence in her returned caress, her eyes open as she watched his face. Together, they collapsed back into the wet sand.

Simon Tyree watched as Billy Starbuck came into the clearing, rifle in hand. There was a pink flush on his cheeks and a strange elation in his eyes. Tyree recognized the look. He had seen it a hundred times on the faces of young men who had just bought their first roll in the sheets and were proud of their foolishness. Tyree's gaze shifted to the young woman beside him. She hardly had the look of a grieving or fretful wife.

"What took you so long?" Tyree drawled. He made no effort to hide his sarcasm. The last thing he needed, if Josiah had indeed survived, was a confrontation between brothers over an opportunistic, conniving female. And in his opinion, Elizabeth Simpson was just that.

Starbuck didn't reply. Properly solicitous, he led Elizabeth to the fire. His arm was around her shoulders, and it remained there, even when they hunkered down in the sand.

Tyree turned to Rebecca. She was wringing out the damp flannel that she would be needing for the baby. "How long has that been going on?" he asked, nodding toward Starbuck and Elizabeth.

Rebecca didn't answer. She simply shook her head and then picked up the baby's basket. Gently, she carried the little boy closer to the warmth of the fire, careful to keep him upwind of the smoke. "Elizabeth," she began.

When the younger woman didn't respond, she tried again. "You've got to watch the baby, Elizabeth," she announced.

Billy Starbuck's face changed. He was torn between the woman beneath his arm and the small infant Rebecca had cradled in the wicker basket. Enraptured, he moved away from Elizabeth, pulling down the corner of the blanket that covered the child. "What's his name, Rebecca?" he said softly. "What's the baby's name?"

The look on the young man's face was one of total captivation, and Rebecca couldn't be angry with him. Nor could she chastise him for his total lack of concern for his brother. After all, *she* had not thought of her husband's well-being until long after she and the baby were safe.

"Benjamin," Rebecca answered softly. When Starbuck reached out to touch the child, she took hold of his wrist. "I want you to help me look for Josiah, Will."

Angry, the young man tried to pull away from her touch. "No," he answered. And then, unable to meet the woman's gaze, he changed his mind. "All right," he said gruffly. Reluctantly, he began to rise.

Elizabeth reached out to him. "Stay with me," she pleaded. She cast a quick eye at her small son and clung to Starbuck's hand even tighter. In all the long months since the little boy's birth, she had never been left alone with him; *she had never wanted to be alone with him*. "Please, Will," she sobbed. "Stay with me and the baby."

Disgusted, Rebecca stood up. She reached for a heavy branch, intending to use it for a torch. It was growing dark, and she would need the light.

"You can use this." Tyree reached out toward her and took the limb, handing her a kerosene lantern to use instead. "We keep them in the rear boot with the repair kit," he explained. His voice lowered. "You haven't eaten yet. There are provisions in the boot, too—and coffee."

Rebecca shook her head. "I've got to . . ." Her brow wrinkled as she tried to find the right words. There were only two possibilities facing her: She would either find Josiah alive, or she would find him dead. "Please help me, Simon," she begged.

Tyree sensed the pain in Rebecca's face. By rights, the woman shouldn't give a damn about her missing husband. In the brief time they had all been together, Tyree had never seen Josiah Simpson treat his elder wife with real affection. "Rebecca . . ." he began.

She silenced him with a single look. "He could be hurt, Simon. I can't bear to think of him—" she paused as she remembered Kyle Lassiter "—of *anyone* lying out there in the cold, alone." Her voice broke.

Tyree took her hand. She had more compassion in the tip of her little finger than Elizabeth had in her entire body. "An hour," he said, looking at the sky. "We'll look for Josiah and Lassiter for an hour." When she started to protest, he shook his head. "It's going to get cold, Rebecca. Too cold for any of us to be outside of that coach."

They moved off into the brush that littered the riverbank. Rebecca's voice lifted in a soft, melancholy way as she called out. "Josiah . . . Josiah!"

Tyree stayed apart from her, concentrating his search on the outer fringe of the light cast by the lantern. It pained him to hear her searching for and calling out to Josiah. Several times he had to remind himself that the man was her husband, and he cursed himself for having gotten involved—in spite of the promise he had made to himself never to let that happen again.

And then, after a fifteen-minute search, he saw a slash of white against the darkness, something wraithlike that hovered just above the ground at the very edge of the river. "Rebecca," he called, "bring the lantern."

She stumbled through the thick, wet brush, angry when Tyree caught her around the waist and held her back. He took the lantern from her. "Stay here," he ordered. She did as she was bid, afraid of what she might find.

Josiah Simpson was firmly lodged on a bed of pine boughs, his body a full foot above the ground. His dark jacket had been torn from him, and the white shirt he wore was wet and plastered to his chest and arms. It was as if he had been lashed to the tree trunk—to the top of the pine tree that had rammed and battered him when he was in the water.

Tyree went down on one knee. Raising the lantern high above the still form, he probed the long artery in the man's neck with his fingers, searching for some sign of a pulse. There was nothing but the cold clamminess of skin that had lost all its warmth and vitality. "Damn," he muttered, thinking of the woman at his back.

Rebecca moved forward. When he tried to stop her with his outstretched arm, she pushed it aside. "Josiah," she murmured, dropping down on her knees and taking the man's hand in hers. She tenderly brushed the dark hair away from his forehead.

At first, Tyree thought she was going to cry. And then she leaned forward, as if she were going to kiss the still form of her husband, her gaze so intent on his face that she was beyond hearing Tyree as he spoke her name. Her head turned, and she laid her ear against Josiah's parted lips, waving Tyree into silence with her free hand. "He's alive," she murmured.

The driver shook his head. "Rebecca . . ."

She wasn't listening. She grabbed Josiah's shoulders, struggling to pull him free from the tangle of pine branches, an incredible strength in her as she almost lifted the man from his perch. Tyree moved to help her, and together they lifted Josiah from his thorny prison and eased him down onto the sand at the edge of the river.

Amazed, the driver watched as Rebecca turned Josiah over onto his stomach. She took great care arranging his arms and his head, her fingers probing into his mouth as she searched for anything that might be obstructing his breathing.

The woman's next moves almost convinced Tyree that she was mad with grief. She straddled Josiah and then, using her palms, began pushing at his back, just below his shoulder blades. Methodically, she continued her strange maneuver, and a thin veil of sweat appeared on her forehead.

Unable to stand this strange charade any longer, he

grabbed Rebecca around her waist in an attempt to pull
her away. "He's gone," he whispered hoarsely in her ear.
When she struggled against him, he repeated the quiet
declaration, phrasing it more strongly. "He's dead!" Rebecca's efforts to escape him only increased. "Listen to
me! *He's dead!*"

Then, as if to prove Tyree wrong, Josiah stirred. A
small cough puffed from between his lips, his shoulders
lifting as a second cough formed deep in his lungs. He
began coughing in earnest, expelling the water he had
swallowed, his body shaking from the effort.

Slowly, Josiah began to rouse from his cold lethargy.
Rebecca was beside him again, briskly rubbing his arms in
an attempt to warm him. Tyree joined her in her efforts.

The revived man took a deep breath. "Elizabeth," he
breathed, the name rasping softly from his sore throat.

Tyree turned the man loose, roughly pushing his arm
away. He turned his eyes on Rebecca and saw a flash of
pain that she was unable to hide. Disgusted, the driver
got up and moved away.

Rebecca was still massaging Josiah's arm. "Elizabeth
is all right," she said softly. She wanted to say more, to
tell Josiah about Starbuck, but she couldn't.

"I'm so cold, Rebecca," Josiah whispered. He was
shaking, the frigid dampness of his clothes weighing him
down.

Tyree returned to the couple. "Can you walk?" he
asked.

The man's teeth were chattering, and it was difficult
for him to speak, but he managed a feeble nod. He tried
to stand, leaning against Rebecca for support.

Tyree slipped beneath Josiah's arm, taking Rebecca's
place. "You carry the lantern," he said, his words harsher
than he had intended. He was angry—angry at Josiah's
disregard for his wife and for Rebecca's caring enough to
be hurt.

The trip back to the campsite took twice as long as
had their original foray in search of Josiah. Three times,
Tyree was forced to stop because Josiah's legs were weak

and rubbery. Night was closing in around them, the canyon void of light except for the lantern Rebecca carried and the feeble glow of the campfire up ahead. As Tyree aimed for the light, he knew they would not be able to search any longer for Kyle Lassiter. Besides, with only one arm, there was little likelihood he could have survived.

Rebecca moved slightly ahead, her pace increasing. Tyree knew the reason for her sudden change in gait: She wanted to warn Starbuck and Elizabeth that Josiah was alive and was coming so that he wouldn't find the young couple embracing. Tyree called out to her, "We need the light, Rebecca." Then in a louder voice, he shouted toward the campfire, "We're coming in!" Maliciously, he almost hoped Starbuck and Elizabeth were taking a tumble in the sand, but fortune denied him.

"Rebecca?" Starbuck came out of the darkness. He stood, his face bathed in the pale glow of the woman's lantern.

Tyree felt a tug under his arm as Josiah came to a sudden halt. The man tensed and then went limp. "Will," he whispered in disbelief.

Starbuck moved forward, his eyes narrowing as he read his brother's lips and the look on his face. "That's right, big brother," he gloated. He thumped his chest with a tightly clenched fist. "Billy Starbuck," he bragged. "*I'm* Billy Starbuck!"

Kyle Lassiter watched the reunion from a grove of pines beyond the fire. Recently arrived, he now had his first good look at the young man who had just declared his identity.

Lassiter's eyes raked the outlaw, the slow appraisal a strange mixture of awe, contempt, and raw rage. He had worked with the young man named Will, had even helped him swamp out stables and harness the teams. And not once had he suspected that the young drifter was anything but what he appeared to be: an irritating, youthful farm kid looking for escape from the harsh realities of the fields.

Unwittingly, his anger clouding his thinking, Lassiter

took a hasty step forward, his gaze fastened on his quarry. A twig snapped beneath his foot, and the sound brought him to his senses. Quickly he withdrew, fading back into the darkness of the drooping pines. He was unarmed; he was unprepared. And the younger man had a rifle.

I've got to wait, he reasoned. *For however long it takes.*

Despite the growing cold, Lassiter began his long vigil. The heat of his anger, his hatred, warmed him. *Tomorrow,* he promised himself. He would find a way tomorrow.

Simon Tyree moved past Billy Starbuck, his arm still around Josiah's upper body. "I'll need that canvas from the rear boot," he said. It wasn't a thought; it was a command.

Tyree's eyes focused on the fire. A coffeepot sat among the coals, a thick cloud of white vapor rising up from the spout. He headed toward the campfire, seeking its warmth, drawn by the aroma of the coffee.

Elizabeth Simpson watched as Tyree and Josiah approached. Her hand flew to her mouth as she stifled a scream, the shock of seeing her husband alive almost too much to bear. She already had begun planning her life without him. Disappointment dulled her features, and she momentarily shrank, but then she recovered. "Josiah!" She rose up and rushed to greet him.

Josiah, still leaning heavily on Tyree for support, opened his arms and held her in an awkward embrace. Tyree eased the man down onto the blanket Elizabeth had just vacated and, without looking at the young woman, gave her a curt order. "He needs a cup of that coffee," he said. "We all do."

Elizabeth's frown returned. She stared at Tyree's harsh profile and then called out, "Rebecca!" The snottiness of her tone made the summons insulting. "Mr. Tyree would like some coffee for himself and for Josiah."

Tyree straightened, his hand darting out to close around the young woman's wrist. "*You* get the coffee!" he ordered, the words coming from between clenched teeth. *"Now!"*

Elizabeth started to argue, and then she saw something in Tyree's face that changed her mind. She turned, lifting her skirts, and marched stiff-backed the short distance to the fire. There was a clatter and a banging of tin against rock as she did as she was told.

Billy Starbuck returned from the coach, the heavy canvas covering from the rear boot draped over his arm. The vision of Elizabeth at the fire warmed him. *That's how it's going to be for us*, he mused. *Elizabeth fussing around the fire while I take care of the important things.*

"The tarp!" Tyree called impatiently, cutting into Starbuck's daydreams. When the young man was slow in responding, Tyree pulled the canvas from his arms, holding it above the fire for a moment, capturing the warmth of the blaze. And then he folded it and placed it over Josiah's shaking shoulders.

They ate a quiet meal, a one-pot dinner cooked from provisions salvaged from the coach. The salt and spices Rebecca had carefully selected before they left Holbrook had been reduced to a useless, wet paste, so the only seasoning came from the single tin of canned meat.

Tyree was the first to finish. He lingered over a final cup of coffee, his mind busy as he considered their plight.

The campsite itself was not too bad. Starbuck had been busy while Tyree and Rebecca were searching for Josiah. He had rigged a rope to tie the horses to and had collected burnable refuse that had washed ashore. He had even had the foresight to hang a line of cord near the fire for drying the wet clothing and blankets from inside the coach. The line now was heavy with sodden goods, and the air filled with the aroma of wet buffalo robes and damp wool.

Still, there was the growing cold. The moon had risen well above the trees, and the air had become bitterly cold. There would be a thin covering of ice on the water come morning.

Starbuck hunkered down next to Tyree's knee. He

held a cup of hot coffee in his hands, relishing the warmth from the tin as he worked it between his palms. "We going to rig a tent?" He nodded at the tarp and the robes that hung steaming on the line beside the fire.

Tyree shook his head. "Everything's too wet. We'd freeze to death while we were sleeping." He tossed the remainder of his coffee into the fire and watched as the liquid danced and sizzled against the hot rocks.

Starbuck rubbed his chin. "With five people and a baby, it'll be a tight squeeze," he said, thinking aloud. There were three seats in the coach, counting the center bench.

"We'll let the women have the two seats," Tyree said and then pointed a finger at Starbuck and Josiah. "The three of us are going to have to make do sitting up."

The idea of being that close to Josiah galled the younger brother. "I'll bunk up on top," he said petulantly and started to rise.

Tyree grabbed his sleeve and pulled him back down. "You listen to me, Will," he said softly. "Whatever's between you and your brother—" his eyes narrowed "—whatever there is between you and me, is going to have to wait until we get out of here."

Starbuck tore away from the man's grip. "You don't know what it was like!" he hissed. "You don't know what Josiah's like, or what he's done to me."

Tyree smiled, but there was no humor in his eyes. "I don't give a damn what he's done to you!" he said truthfully, and then he thought, *Whatever it was, it wasn't as bad as what you've done to him.* He was thinking of Elizabeth and what he knew had occurred between the younger Simpson and his sister-in-law before he brought her to the campsite. "All I care about is getting out of here." The baby started to cry. "And getting that baby out of here. If you can't keep yourself in check, then you think about that baby, and about that little . . ." He hesitated. "About his mother. And Rebecca," he finished softly.

Starbuck digested Simon Tyree's words. He knew the man was right, but the knowledge didn't dull his anger.

And then he thought of the strongbox and the things it would buy for him and Elizabeth and their child.

Tyree recognized the gleam of greed in the outlaw's eye. "Not hardly, boy," he said cryptically.

Starbuck stared at Tyree. "What?" he asked.

But Tyree did not answer. He stood up, stretched, and simply walked away.

Chapter Ten

Kyle Lassiter listened and watched from his vantage place in the darkness beyond the circle of light cast by the campfire. The cold had driven Tyree and the others inside the coach, and the only noises now were the fatigued and muffled coughings of the five people as they settled in and the restless snorting and head tossing of the tethered horses.

The animals drew Lassiter's immediate attention. Two of them, the large bays that belonged to Navaho Stage Line, stood side by side, whickering softly, as if finding solace in each other's company.

A third horse stood aloof from the heavier dray animals. The mare was finer in conformation than were the coach horses and a full two hands shorter. She was long legged and broad of chest, clearly bred for speed as well as endurance, yet sturdy enough to carry a man over a long distance. *Even in rough terrain*, Lassiter thought, thinking of the times Billy Starbuck had eluded capture. Riding the horse, he surmised, must have been akin to riding the wind.

Taking a quick last look at the coach, Lassiter walked to where the horses were tied. He came in slowly, heading first for the two coach horses, knowing they would recognize his scent and be less apt to spook. He spoke to them softly, his gloved hand sliding along the rope as he

moved toward the horses' heads. "Easy," he crooned, his
voice barely audible. "Easy, now." The animals responded,
stretching out their noses to accept the man's touch. He
only paused a moment, scratching one and then the other,
his eyes reserved for the little black mare.

Ducking under the necks of the two bays, Lassiter
carefully reached out to the animal and then glanced at
the saddle Starbuck had left in place. His hand reached
across and touched the empty rifle scabbard, and his smile
faded slightly as he realized the young outlaw had not
been foolish enough to leave his weapon behind unat-
tended.

Stepping to the front of the animal, Lassiter stroked
the velvet softness of her muzzle. Up close, the horse was
even more impressive, well muscled and obviously grain
fed. There was a bright sheen to her coat, which had just
begun to shed its winter fur. Checking her teeth, Lassiter
judged her age at about five. She was a horse worth
having, he mused. If nothing else, Starbuck was an excel-
lent judge of horseflesh.

Thinking of the young outlaw, Lassiter's face hardened. He was truly sorry that Tyree had gotten in the
way of his shooting Starbuck earlier, but that would not
deter him. One way or the other, he would have his
revenge.

But first he would need a weapon. With a rifle or
revolver, he could simply walk up to the coach and take
the sleeping occupants by surprise. It would be a simple
matter, especially since they thought he was dead. He
would then merely announce that he was taking his prisoner on to Flagstaff and would send back a fresh team of
horses for Tyree and the others. Tyree might object—he
might even know Lassiter had no intention of bringing in
Starbuck alive—but there would be little he could do
without a gun.

Keeping hold of the mare's reins, Lassiter untied her
and led her behind the two coach horses, taking his time
as he pulled the slack cinch tight and struggled to make
the necessary knot. Pausing, he thought about turning the

two remaining animals loose, but then decided he would not; they would only follow after him, leaving a trail that Tyree and the others could use to track him. It would be better to make it look like the mare had worked her way loose and wandered off, just as it would be better to let Tyree continue to think that he was dead.

Lassiter took his time, allowing the mare to forage a bit before leading her farther away from the others. She would take a mouthful of grass, and while she was chewing, Lassiter would lead her to another clump of new graze. Patiently, he continued working away from the coach horses, until finally he mounted the mare and started upstream.

Lassiter knew where he could obtain a rifle. It was only a few miles upriver and across to Devil's Canyon Station. But as he continued upstream along the river-bank, he realized there was another, far better place to get a gun. It would take only a few hours to ride beyond Devil's Canyon to the next station down the line—at Clear Creek. There he would find not only a weapon, but fresh horses and the railroad payroll. He could have it all—Billy Starbuck and the gold—and no one would be the wiser.

Simon Tyree reluctantly placed himself between Josiah Simpson and his brother on the narrow center bench of the stagecoach. He felt doubly confined: held fast by the shoulders of the two men and almost overwhelmed by their hostility toward each other. The women had gone to sleep, but that did not stop the two men from bickering, their whispered words so intense they seemed to be shouting.

Josiah's anger was righteous. He began with a sermon filled with quotes from the Book of Proverbs. There was a pompous air of superiority about him as he lectured his younger brother on the ways of evil.

Starbuck took it until he could stand it no longer. "Just shut up!" he hissed. Knowing an oath would infuriate his brother even more, he repeated the words. "Goddamn it, Josiah! Just shut up!"

Tyree felt Josiah suddenly go rigid. The man mumbled something about sparing the rod, and then, reaching across in front of Tyree, he swung.

Starbuck ducked the blow and grabbed at his brother's hand, holding it firmly in his own as he tried to rise up off the seat, intent on breaking Josiah's arm. He twisted and lifted straight up at the same time, a quick, vicious movement that almost tipped the narrow bench he was now straddling.

Still seated between the two brothers, Tyree was growing angry. Starbuck's stomach loomed in his face, and he could feel Josiah's soft belly at his side. Using both arms, Tyree suddenly erupted, ramming an elbow into Josiah's vulnerable belly, at the same time delivering a stout fist into Starbuck's. Both men collapsed back onto the seat.

"Jesus," Starbuck breathed, gasping for breath as he rubbed his sore stomach. Josiah said nothing.

Tyree took advantage of the sudden truce to do his own sermonizing. "No more," he said ominously, lowering his voice when he saw Rebecca stir restlessly. His tone made it clear to both men that he would stand for no more of their feuding.

Starbuck withdrew into the bitter memories of his childhood. Not for one moment did he give up his plan to avenge himself on his domineering brother, no matter what Tyree had threatened. *I can wait, old man*, he thought, glancing at his rifle propped beside him against the door, his rage finding a new direction as he thought of Tyree's interference. *You have no idea how long or how well I can wait*. And then he nodded off to sleep.

Tyree was still tense. Josiah was making prayerful mutterings in his right ear, but they were not as troubling as the snores on his left. Starbuck was leaning against the leeward door, sound asleep, his body compacted like a napping panther, his arm wrapped protectively around the barrel of his rifle.

"What happened between you and your brother?"

Tyree said softly, addressing Josiah. He didn't know if he really cared or if he was just fighting sleep.

Josiah's murmurings stopped. "Nothing," he replied after a short silence. In his pious mind, it was inconceivable that he could have done anything wrong, anything that could have contributed to his young brother's descent into a life of crime.

Tyree exhaled loudly. He tried a different approach. "Then what did he do to you?"

Josiah's back stiffened again as he struggled to find an adequate answer. "He defied me," the man said sternly. "From the day our father died, he defied me." He lapsed into a short silence, then said bitterly, "From the time the boy was ten he had a streak of spoiled independence— impudence—and I vowed to tame him. But his evil nature resisted my authority."

Tyree shook his head. There was, he judged, a good twenty years difference in age between Josiah and Starbuck—enough of a difference that the two men were in all likelihood linked only by blood. Suddenly, he no longer cared. If they were fool enough to behave like Cain and Abel, then so be it.

Tyree drifted off into a troubled sleep. He spent a long night fighting dream demons: the weather, the noise of the water in the rolling river that assaulted his mind even while he slept. But most of all he fought the image of Josiah and Will Simpson as they fought each other, dooming everyone to a slow death in the depths of Devil's Canyon.

The next morning Billy Starbuck was the first to rise. He opened the coach door to a strange, eerie world of silver and gray. A frigid mist hovered over the terrain, with ice crystallized on the ground and the lower branches of the pines, a thin crust of hoarfrost covering everything.

Rifle in hand, Starbuck stumbled out into the dawn, shivering against the damp cold as he scurried toward the smoldering embers of the campfire. He raked at the coals with a wet limb, his teeth chattering as he stirred up a small flame. He thought of the warmth in his small cabin, but that had to remain his secret.

He went about his chores, concentrating on the fire and the immediate need for coffee. Mold had already started to form on the bag of ground coffee that Rebecca had purchased in Holbrook, and the young man took great care in his efforts to salvage the remainder. The brew would be weak, but it would be hot.

Soon Tyree joined the outlaw at the fire. He stretched, ruefully noting Starbuck's fleeting grin when his stiff joints cracked. "Your time will come soon enough," Tyree observed dryly. "If you live long enough to get this old." In spite of himself, he could not really dislike the outlaw or envy him his youth.

Starbuck laughed. "Oh, I'll live, old man." He winked, pointing his rifle at the driver's boot of the coach where the strongbox still sat. "Long and well." He poured Tyree a cup of the boiled coffee and handed it to him before taking his own.

Tyree observed Starbuck thoughtfully, more puzzled than before by the animosity between him and his brother. It was, he surmised, the woman, Josiah's second wife.

Clearly, it was not that the young man was hesitant to work. The previous night he had done a good job of establishing their campsite—collecting firewood, seeing to it the horses were properly tethered. . . . Tyree's eyes swung to where the horse had been tied.

Something was wrong. He stared off into the mist and realized at once that they were shy one horse. Gesturing with his cup, he said softly to the young man, "The mare is gone."

Starbuck turned. His mouth dropped open. He had not unsaddled the mare the night before, choosing instead to loosen her cinch and let her stand at ready. It was an old habit of the outlaw's, one that was hard to break. "Damn!" he swore.

The two men started toward the tie rope. "You sure you tied her off?" Tyree asked.

Starbuck nodded vigorously. "Every damned bit as

good as those two," he answered, pointing to the two bays. His voice carried a bit of annoyance; the young man was hurt that Tyree could think him so irresponsible about something that was so important. "I tied her off," he said softly.

Tyree ducked under the rope, searching for some sign that the little black had torn free. There was nothing. He checked the leather straps that secured the two dray animals. The knots were secure, looped twice around the rope in a tight figure eight. He pointed to one of the knots for the younger man's inspection. "You tie her up like this?"

Again, the outlaw's head bobbed up and down with great vigor. And then, crestfallen, he reconsidered. "I don't know," he said honestly. Once, during a long stay at the cabin, for want of something to do, he had trained the mare to use her teeth to pull free of a slipknot. It had required no special gift on the mare's part; he had simply rewarded her with molasses candy when she freed herself at his bidding. Horses, he knew, were creatures of great curiosity and like small children were easily bored. If out of habit he had tied her with his usual slipknot, it was conceivable that sometime during the long night she had pulled the strap loose and simply drifted away.

Again, the young man swore. "Damn. *Goddamn!*" Not only had he lost his mount, but his saddle, bridle, and cartridges for his Winchester were gone. And, he remembered belatedly, so were the six sticks of dynamite and blasting caps still packed in his saddlebags.

Tyree saw the look on the man's face and assumed that it was the loss of his ammunition that he mourned as much as the loss of his horse. "Makes us sort of even," he said.

"What do you mean?" Starbuck asked.

"We're both weaponless," Tyree replied with a slight grin, knowing that Starbuck had no idea he had a revolver in the coach, hidden in the inside pocket of his heavy jacket. Seeing the look of confusion as the young outlaw stared at the Winchester in his own hands, Tyree continued, "Have you checked your rifle this morning?"

Starbuck quickly levered the weapon and opened the chamber. It was empty.

"You sleep mighty heavy, son. Not good for *desperado*. I emptied it a couple of hours ago, and I just finished tossing the bullets in the river." It was all Tyree could do to contain his laughter.

With a flash of anger and embarrassment in his eyes, Starbuck threw the rifle back toward the coach. Then he spun around and stared in the direction he thought his mare had wandered. "She'll come back," he finally muttered, his mind more on the box of cartridges than on the horse. "If not here, then—" Realizing his blunder, he stopped midsentence.

Tyree did not miss a word—even the unspoken ones. "Then *where?*" he asked pointedly.

Lips tight, Starbuck refused to answer.

Tyree turned back to the campfire, where Rebecca was preparing breakfast and Josiah was helping himself to the coffee. Elizabeth, he assumed, was still inside the coach. "We've got to find the other horses," he said, thinking of the two from his team that might have survived the river. Looking at the outlaw, he said, "The *coach* horses."

"Sure," Starbuck snorted, nothing agreeable in his answer. "Why not?" He turned and marched back to the fire.

Tyree stared after the young man. The outlaw's changing moods were enough to drive a saint to drink. One moment he was helpful, seemingly concerned; the next he was distant, selfishly uncommunicative, as if he lived in an alien world, totally apart from the needs of anyone else. Disgusted, Tyree drained his mug of coffee. "To hell with it!" he mused. He wasn't going to waste any more of his time worrying; he would do what he could to get out of this canyon and back on the road to Flagstaff.

*   *   *

Hidden among the trees on a slight rise less than a hundred yards from the campsite, Kyle Lassiter sat on the black mare, grinning as he watched the others finish their breakfast. In tow behind him were two stage horses from the Clear Creek way station. One was saddled—it would first bear Billy Starbuck to meet his maker and then would provide a fresh mount for himself. The second bore three saddlebags stuffed with the gold and paper currency he had hidden at the station with Tyree. It had been an easy night's work to obtain a rifle, ammunition, the horses, and the treasure. It was a shame, however, that Owen Parsons had interfered. Lassiter had not intended to kill the old man, but now that it was over, perhaps it was for the best, he thought. Just as it might be best if he alone left Devil's Canyon alive.

Lassiter grinned as he thought of the dynamite he had found in the saddlebag of Starbuck's horse. It was just what he needed to give him the advantage against the guns of Tyree and the outlaw. As he sat on his horse and watched the activity at the coach, he reviewed his plan. He knew that it was only a question of time before Tyree set out to find the two coach horses that might have survived the hell in the river. The driver needed those two animals, along with the pair Starbuck had stolen from the Devil's Canyon way station, if he planned on getting the big Concord rolling and out of the canyon.

There was no other way for Tyree, Lassiter reasoned. The presence of the two women and the infant prevented the driver from simply riding out. Besides, he knew Tyree well enough to recognize the fact that he would consider himself a failure if he had to abandon the coach—or if he returned to Flagstaff without the outlaw in tow. Starbuck's capture would justify, in Tyree's mind, the jeopardy in which he had placed his passengers. After all, the driver was a man of principle, and that fact filled Lassiter with a sense of great pleasure. Tyree would be absolutely determined to get everyone, and everything to the end of the line.

Lassiter continued to wait. When the time was right—

when Tyree and Starbuck were off in search of the other horses—he would make his move to take Josiah Simpson, the women, and the infant hostage. Having seen the outlaw's reactions to Elizabeth and Rebecca, Lassiter firmly believed that Starbuck would do anything, *anything*, to keep his family from being harmed.

A trade, Lassiter mused. He was going to offer Tyree a trade. Billy Starbuck in exchange for the four members of his family. If that failed, he would kill them all.

Patiently, Lassiter watched as Tyree helped clean up the litter from the morning meal. He seemed, Lassiter thought, especially solicitous of the older woman, going out of his way to help her with her chores. *Interesting*, the guard thought; he hadn't envisioned the driver as the sort to be so domesticated.

It was true. Tyree was especially attentive. He had watched Rebecca through the morning as she divided her time between cooking their meal and fretting over the baby. There were dark circles under her eyes.

Rebecca's concern for the baby was not unfounded. The child, seemingly snug and warm in his wicker bed, was listless, too quiet. He lay almost motionless beneath the flannel coverings in the basket, occasionally whimpering. His breath came in short, wet gasps, and Rebecca, fearing the worst, found it harder and harder to keep her mind on her morning chores.

Tyree watched as, for what seemed like the hundredth time, Rebecca returned to the basket to feel the little boy's forehead. He joined her, covering her hand with his own, his brow furrowing as he heard the wet rattle that emanated from the baby's small chest. "What is it, Rebecca?" he murmured.

She hesitated. "He's sick, Simon. He's very sick."

Josiah overheard his wife's words. Forgetting his own weakness, he joined her, immediately seeing Tyree's hand still in place atop Rebecca's on Benjamin's forehead. "What's wrong?" he asked quietly.

Rebecca chose her words carefully. Josiah had waited

a long time for this child, and in spite of his uneasiness in handling the infant, he was genuinely fond of the boy—as fond as a man like Josiah could be. "Benjamin's ill, Josiah," she said. She didn't need to say any more.

Josiah was visibly alarmed. He closed his eyes and scowled. They were stuck in the middle of nowhere, held prisoner by circumstance and the same river that had almost destroyed them. There was no medicine and no real shelter where they could look after the infant. Worse, there was no hope for rescue. "My God, Rebecca," he sighed weakly.

Billy Starbuck wandered over and joined the gathering. For Elizabeth's sake, he had remained aloof from the infant, not yet wanting to let Josiah know the truth about who the little boy's real father was. Trying hard to remain nonchalant, he reached out to touch Rebecca's arm. She responded before he had a chance to speak.

"The baby is sick, Will. Very sick." The helplessness in her voice was devastating.

"I can go for help," Starbuck offered, his own panic growing. He gestured toward the two coach horses that were still tied at the edge of camp. "I can take one of the horses, ride for . . ." In his confusion, he hesitated. It was as far, almost, to Holbrook as it was to Flagstaff. And he had done a thorough job of seeing to it that no telegraph was available at the stations in between. For the first time, the young man was truly ashamed of what he had done. He fell silent.

Tyree was already busy. "We'll have to make do with the coach," he said, knowing there was little else available to them. He estimated the size of the canvas tarp drying beside the fire. "We can rig a canopy over the door and build a fire closer to the Concord." The task of properly sheltering the baby seemed hopeless; he could provide a reasonable amount of heat for the infant, but could do very little about the killing dampness, the still-wet canvas and heavy buffalo robes. There was absolutely nothing he could do about the medicine they didn't have.

"My cabin," Starbuck said quietly. All eyes turned

toward him. "I've got a cabin," he continued. "It's about a half mile from here, downriver."

Dumbfounded, Tyree and the others stared at the young man. No one said anything.

Then Elizabeth, still half asleep, emerged from the coach. She had been inside listening, too selfish in her own need for warmth and comfort to be concerned about her child. "How could you!" she raged. She stepped down from the Concord and went directly to Starbuck. Confronting him, she continued her tirade. "I spent a miserable night inside that coach, freezing, without so much as a dry blanket for comfort, and *you* have a cabin!" Unable to control herself any longer, she struck out at the young man, her fists beating against his chest.

He grabbed her hands. "Beth!" Still holding her, he drew her close, no longer caring if Josiah saw. "I *couldn't* tell, Beth," he said softly so the others wouldn't hear. "I was waiting until I had the money. Until I could take you away."

Speechless, Elizabeth collapsed against Starbuck's chest. The thought of what the money would mean to her was all it took to make her forgive him.

He patted her shoulder and, with his arm still around her waist, again faced Tyree and the others. "We can make it. Rebecca and Elizabeth can take the baby and ride." His brow smoothed as he begrudgingly reconsidered. "Josiah, too, if he has to. I can lead one horse, and you can lead the other."

Too angry to say anything, Tyree only nodded. He started toward the horses, reaching out to grab Starbuck's arm as he passed him and almost dragging the outlaw along beside him.

They quickly readied the two horses. The women would have to straddle the broad backs of the dray animals, with little regard for comfort or modesty. Tyree and Starbuck would have the harsh chore of leading two reluctant horses trained to the harness—not for riding through the ankle-deep sand and silt at the river's edge.

There was the matter of Josiah Simpson, too. Putting

him astride a horse with Elizabeth would only aggravate the angry feelings between Josiah and his younger brother; yet Tyree felt there was no alternative. Josiah was still weak, but he was better able than Elizabeth to deal with a horse that had no desire to be ridden.

"I'm going to put your brother and Elizabeth on the same mount," Tyree growled at the young outlaw beside him. "You're going to lead that horse, and you're going to make damned sure that nothing happens. I'll be right behind you every damned step of the way. Understand?"

Starbuck said nothing. His jaw tightened, but he accepted Tyree's words without argument. He would wait, and when the time was right, he would act. *I'll show you, old man*, he thought. *Before this is over, I'll show you. Just like I'm going to show Josiah.*

The young man stepped away from the horse he had been blanketing with a makeshift buffalo-robe saddle. "I'm ready," he announced, purposely avoiding Tyree's eyes as he struggled to regain control of his temper.

Tyree studied the outlaw's face, catching the brief glimpse of hot anger that flashed in the pale eyes. He remembered what Starbuck had said to Elizabeth about the money, but the knowledge that the money was hidden at the Clear Creek station gave him no satisfaction; as far as Starbuck was concerned, the money was still in the strongbox.

For a moment, Tyree was tempted to tell the outlaw that the money was gone, that he no longer had it with him. But he knew that would be a mistake. It wouldn't take long for the young man to realize where the gold was, and even less time for him to try taking the horses and Elizabeth.

Tyree had no other choice but to continue the sham. He helped Rebecca onto the big bay gelding, handing her the baby. Then he secured the strongbox behind, balancing it across the horse's back, aware the whole time that he was being watched by the smiling young outlaw. *Damn you*, Tyree cursed silently. *Goddamn you!*

* * *

Kyle Lassiter watched with alarm as Simon Tyree and Billy Starbuck prepared to lead the two horses out of the canyon. He had not expected this: a foolhardy attempt to make the long walk to Flagstaff. Then he realized that the two men were pointing the horses south—and Flagstaff lay northwest of the canyon.

A slow smile of understanding formed on Lassiter's lips, his mood improving. He waited until Tyree and the others were out of sight, and then he leisurely began to follow in their wake, their clear trail marring the wet sand. When the small mare he was riding—Starbuck's horse—perked up and increased her gait, Lassiter's smile grew; the horse already knew where she was going. He pulled her up, slowing her pace, and wound the reins around the horn, sure that the horse was going home.

Chapter Eleven

The cabin loomed before them, a welcome sight as Simon Tyree followed Billy Starbuck up a slight incline and into the small clearing. A man more suited to riding than walking, Tyree was plagued by a dull cramping ache in his legs and a sharper, more intense pain in his lungs. Still, his main concern was for the woman mounted on the horse he was leading and for the infant boy cradled in her arms. Finally they reached the front door.

Tyree reached up to Rebecca, gently taking her in his arms as he lifted her down from the horse's broad back. The baby was between them, and Tyree paused just long enough to touch Benjamin's flushed cheek. Then he tethered the horse to a tree not far from the cabin and lifted the strongbox off the back of the animal.

After tying off the other horse, Billy Starbuck rudely pushed past Tyree, opened the door, and stood back as Elizabeth flounced across the threshold. Tyree said nothing at her bold selfishness, silently reminding himself that she, not Rebecca, was Benjamin's mother. The thought was intended to evoke a feeling of compassion toward the young woman; instead it caused him to shake his head in disgust. Elizabeth Simpson didn't deserve a child, any more than she deserved even the slightest consideration.

"Go ahead, Rebecca," he said softly, nodding toward

119

the open door. Carrying the strongbox, he followed her inside.

The interior of the cabin came as a pleasant surprise. There was a neatness, a sense of home to the place, the stout walls forming a barrier that halted the wet, cold breeze that blew across the river. Starbuck began building a fire in the wide hearth, and almost immediately the pleasant aroma of dry pinecones filled the single room.

Rebecca laid the little boy on the narrow bed. The wetness of his clothing—the small squares of flannel she had used to cover him—alarmed her. It was more than the dampness caused by the river; it was the child's own feverish sweat. She shook her head, her eyes searching the small cabin for something—*anything*—that would help her tend to the infant's immediate needs.

As if he could read her mind, Starbuck appeared and held out the top half of a clean pair of long johns, as well as a soft flannel shirt. "Here," he said softly.

Gratefully, Rebecca took the dry clothing, undressed Benjamin—appalled by the cold clamminess of his plump legs and arms—and wrapped him in the dry cloth. She felt totally helpless and, in spite of the others, strangely alone.

Tyree was going through the cabinet above the small dry sink. The shelves held enough canned goods, dried meat, and beans to feed one man for the better part of a long winter and well into the summer. He suppressed a smile, refusing to let Starbuck know that he was impressed by such foresight, and then turned to face the younger man. "Plenty of food," he began, nodding at the full shelves. His voice lowered, and he made no effort to hide the sarcasm. "It's just too bad, considering your line of work, that you weren't smart enough to figure that you might need a decent store of medical supplies, too." Tyree was thinking of the posses that had pursued Starbuck after the robberies, and the amount of lead that had been fired at him.

Staring directly into Tyree's eyes, Starbuck tapped one of the small drawers beneath the bed with the toe of his boot, then reached down and pulled at the knob. "I think you'll find everything you need, Rebecca," he said arrogantly, never taking his gaze off Tyree's face.

Rebecca stared at the contents of the drawer. It was an exact duplicate of the one in her own kitchen that she had always kept filled with the medicinal items needed in an isolated frontier home. Everything was the same, from the soft supply of clean linen bandages to the green glass bottles of patent medicines, apothecary powders, and ointments. She reached into the drawer, knowing that she would find the camphorated oil in exactly the same place she had kept her own; she was not disappointed. "I'll need a small pot of boiling water," she said softly. "And a second kettle for his bottle."

Tyree nodded and went outside to the horses. When he returned, he was carrying the bundle of baby things Rebecca had brought with her from the coach.

Together, Tyree, Josiah, and Rebecca worked to make the little boy comfortable. Josiah had emptied a second drawer from beneath the bed, lining it with Starbuck's clean clothing. He placed Benjamin inside, carried the makeshift crib to the table, and then, with Tyree's help, moved the table closer to the fire. The cast-iron pot of water was already boiling, the pungent scent of camphor and eucalyptus rising up with the steam to fill the air and Benjamin's small, congested lungs.

For the first time since breakfast, Rebecca began to relax. The warmth of the fire brought more than a degree of comfort to her aching arms and back. There was a feeling of safety in this place, and she welcomed it.

Josiah reached out and touched her arm, bringing her back to reality. He watched as she prepared a bottle of medicated sugar water for the child, grateful that she was there but unable to express what he was feeling. "And now?" he asked softly.

Rebecca exhaled. "We wait, Josiah. All we can do is wait. We have Will to thank for this shelter," she said, giving a single nod that encompassed the entire room. She was genuinely grateful for the younger man's help and for his willingness to bring them to a place that he obviously considered special, a place that was his alone.

Josiah's jaw tensed, and he nodded his head. "Just like we have him to thank for everything that's happened," he said bitterly. His tone was utterly unforgiving.

Briefly, Rebecca closed her eyes. "He didn't have to bring us here, Josiah," she argued quietly. It was the truth, and she wanted desperately for Josiah to acknowledge it. "He could have left us at the river, without even trying to help." *It's just like it's always been,* she thought sadly. *No matter what Will did or how hard he tried, it was never enough for Josiah.* It was no small wonder that he had finally quit trying and had run away.

Angrily—stubbornly—Josiah shook his head. "He'll never change, Rebecca. He's just like he's always been: willful, unrepentant, and spoiled." Josiah had not forgotten how his middle-aged parents had doted on their "surprise" child or the amount of time and attention they had lavished on him. "And damned," he finished, his voice carrying—as he intended for it to carry.

Billy Starbuck's head came up, his face suddenly white. He started across the room, only to find his way barred by Simon Tyree.

"The horses," Tyree said, standing his ground. He had put on his heavy jacket, the Remington pistol heavy and comfortably out of sight inside the inner pocket. "You're going to help me find the other horses."

There was a long, tense moment as the younger man considered Tyree's words. And then he smiled. "Not yet," he breathed, shaking his head. He was still looking past Tyree at his elder brother.

Tyree took the outlaw's arm and ushered him toward the door. "Don't push it," he warned.

Starbuck laughed. He pulled away from Tyree just long enough to take a startled Elizabeth Simpson in his arms. The kiss was long, filled with a young man's passion, and meant more to devil his brother than to impress Elizabeth.

"You bastard!" Josiah roared. He lunged across the

room, his fingers clawing wildly at the air as Tyree quickly
jerked open the door and shoved Starbuck outside.

"You little fool!" Tyree rasped as he slammed the
door shut.

Again, Billy Starbuck laughed. "I'm going to take
her," he promised, shouting the words so that Josiah could
hear. He danced away·from Tyree, yelling the words at
the closed door. "You hear me, Josiah? When this is over,
I'm going to take Elizabeth, just like I'm going to take my
s—"

Anticipating his words, Tyree grabbed the outlaw and
clapped a gloved hand over his mouth, twisting his arm as
he propelled him across the clearing. They made it as far
as the river's edge.

Lassiter sat astride the black mare, only partially hidden among the pines, the way-station rifle resting across
the pommel with the stock wedged beneath his right
elbow. The forefinger of his hand was wrapped around the
trigger. "Simon," he greeted pleasantly. His smile was
almost cordial.

Shocked to see Lassiter alive, Tyree stopped dead in
his tracks. He quickly recovered, nodding his head in
greeting, his fingers still clenched around Billy Starbuck's
upper arm. "Kyle."

Still smiling, Lassiter's eyes drifted slowly to the young
man at Tyree's side, the rifle following his gaze as it swung
into a direct line with Starbuck's head. "Been a long time
coming, boy," he breathed.

Tyree studied Lassiter's profile, still amazed that he
had not drowned. "I didn't think you'd made it," he said,
uncomfortably aware of the man's strange composure.

Lassiter laughed, the sound bitter and filled with
rancor. "Did you even bother to look?" he asked finally.

"I wasn't going to. There didn't seem to be much
point, Kyle," he observed honestly. "But we searched
until dark. Rebecca insisted." Carefully, he took a single
step backward, dragging Billy Starbuck with him.

"I want Starbuck, Tyree," Lassiter said softly, nudg-
ing the black mare, urging her a single pace ahead.

Tyree shook his head. "I need him, Kyle. Until we get out of here, I need him." It was the truth.

Lassiter snorted. He didn't give a damn what Tyree needed. Not anymore. "You need him as much as you need *them*?" he countered. Using the barrel of the rifle, he gestured toward the stand of pines at his back.

Tyree stared along the barrel of the rifle, his gaze coming to rest on the dark shadows beneath the trees. "The horses," he said. "But they're not—"

Lassiter nodded. "That's right. They're not the missing horses. I got these fellows last night—at the Clear Creek station." He paused, allowing the full impact of the words to hit home, then continued. "Starbuck for the horses," he bargained, careful to keep himself between the tethered animals and the driver.

Tyree felt Starbuck tense beneath his fingers and instinctively sensed that the young man was feeling a sense of dread, as if he knew he was facing something more terrible than death. The feeling made the skin on Tyree's neck crawl, but he forced a smile. "Come with us, Kyle," he suggested. "You can turn Starbuck in to the marshal at Flagstaff. He paused and then added, "And we can deliver the railroad payroll."

Lassiter shook his head. "I'm taking him in alone."

As if he were too warm, Tyree unbuttoned his coat. "On one horse, Kyle?" he asked pointedly. Somehow, he had known all along that the man had no intention of leaving the two horses.

Lassiter's lips compressed in a tight line, his eyes narrowing as he surveyed Tyree. "I've no quarrel with you, Simon. I'll send someone back with a fresh team," he lied. "Soon as I get to Flagstaff, I'll send someone back."

The driver shook his head. "But you're not going to Flagstaff, are you, Kyle?" he said softly.

Lassiter was losing control, just as he was losing patience. "I can simply *take* him, Simon," he threatened quietly. To make his point, he swung the barrel of the Winchester down and to the side, centering it in a direct line with Tyree's belly.

Suddenly, the driver pulled Starbuck in front of him, using the outlaw's body to shield the movement of his right hand. He drew the Remington, shoving the weapon between Starbuck's elbow and side, and pointed it at Kyle Lassiter's chest. "It's a standoff, Kyle," he said, the words barely above a whisper as he took another full step backward, pulling the younger man along with him. He cocked the pistol, knowing full well that Lassiter could never fire his rifle and reload for a second shot before Tyree blew him out of the saddle.

Billy Starbuck, however, was not so wise, nor did he fully comprehend what was happening. With Lassiter's rifle pointed at his midsection, and Tyree's pistol—*how the hell could he have forgotten Tyree's Remington?* —dangerously close to his ribs, the young man panicked. He felt the fear of impending death and reacted accordingly. Jamming his elbow tight against his side, he whirled around, tearing the pistol from Tyree's hand. The Remington discharged, the bullet scorching the inside sleeve of Starbuck's shirt and burning a long path beneath his lower rib. Crying out, Starbuck belly flopped to the ground.

Tyree dove across the outlaw's back, scrambling to retrieve the pistol. A slug tore into the dirt beside his head, and he swore. Grabbing the weapon, he rolled over and away, firing twice as he spun across the sand. The loud sound of metal working against metal came as Lassiter cocked the rifle and poised to fire again.

Tyree kept rolling. His third shot went high, and he saw a puff of dust as the bullet skimmed across the left shoulder of Lassiter's heavy poncho. Cursing, the guard struggled with the rifle and the reins, hanging on tightly to the saddle horn as the black mare bolted and shied away. The horse wheeled around, almost unseating its rider, and then galloped off into the thick brush.

Not wanting to waste his shots, Tyree stopped firing and found cover among the scattering of rocks that dotted the riverbank. He called out to the young man who lay on the ground. "Will!"

Cautiously, Billy Starbuck lifted his head. He was

able to see the driver, just as he was able to see the two horses Lassiter had tied off to the lower branches of the pines just beyond the clearing. Remaining still, the young man probed the dark shadows beyond the trees, his eyes searching for some sign of Lassiter and the black mare. Satisfied that they were not there, he rose up on his hands and knees and, hugging the ground, darted off into the trees.

Tyree watched the outlaw sprint into the darkness beneath the evergreens. He sucked in a lungful of air and held his breath in anticipation, applauding Starbuck's bravado while cursing his stupidity. It was becoming obvious that the young man had more luck than he had brains.

Grinning, Starbuck raced back across the sandy riverbank, the two horses trotting behind him. Feet first, he slid into place beside Tyree. "Well, I got us the horses, old man!" he declared proudly.

Before Tyree could answer, there was the sound of shot, the rock above his head exploded, and a rain of granite shards peppered both Tyree and the younger man at his side. The horses panicked, screaming in terror as the needlelike pieces of rock bit into their necks and shoulders. Starbuck, still holding on to the reins, was jerked upright and lifted clear off the ground. "Son of a bitch!" he swore incredulously.

Unable to help himself, Tyree laughed. He fired into the pines, waving Starbuck away from him. "You got 'em, all right!" he shouted. "Now let's see you keep 'em!"

Starbuck placed himself between the bays and sprinted toward a tree not far from the cabin, where in an instant he secured the horses' reins. Tyree followed behind the horses, firing into the trees as he moved. Together, the two men raced through the cabin door. They slammed it shut, just as two shots followed in remarkably quick succession, the first bullet thunking against the thick planks, the second hitting the iron hinge and ricocheting across the face of the heavy metal.

"Lassiter's alive. He wants Will," Tyree said, seeing the look on Josiah's face. He brushed past the man and closed the heavy shutters on the windows facing the river. The long gun slots in each window seemed to mock him; there were more gun ports than there were guns. "One to one," he said softly, sorry now that Starbuck's empty rifle was back at the coach, but grateful that Lassiter had nothing more than the rifle.

Starbuck was at Tyree's side. He helped secure the shutters, lifting the heavy iron bar and slipping it into place. "He's got the dynamite," he said softly, not looking at Tyree.

"What?"

The younger man swallowed and said, "There were six sticks of dynamite in my saddlebags."

"Goddamn!" Tyree swore loudly. He slammed the flats of his hands hard against the shutters, his jaw aching as he clamped it shut. He faced the outlaw, trying hard to control his temper and not knowing why he should make the effort. "Is there anything else you'd care to tell me?" he breathed, a biting sarcasm adding an edge to his words.

Starbuck nodded. "There's dynamite, blasting caps, matches, and plenty of fuse," he replied, the words coming as if he were a penitent making his last confession.

"Dynamite!" Elizabeth Simpson shrieked, her voice much the same as it was when she had faced the horror of the river. "He has dynamite!" And then she began to scream, her high-pitched wails intensified by the closeness of the four walls. They were soon echoed by the fretful cries of the startled baby.

Starbuck reached out to console Elizabeth, his hand colliding with his brother's. Still crying, the young woman pulled away from both men, retreating to a far corner and coyly waiting for one of them—it didn't matter which—to follow and offer her comfort. When neither moved, she began crying louder.

Rebecca could stand it no longer. She grabbed Elizabeth, one hand on each shoulder. "Stop it!" she ordered. When Elizabeth's weeping continued even more loudly than before, Rebecca slapped her, the single blow bringing a shocked, abrupt silence.

Elizabeth cowered against the wall, her face livid, the marks of Rebecca's fingers a dark crimson across her cheek. She rubbed at the soreness, feeling the welts. "You hate me!" she rasped. "I took Josiah away from you and gave him a son, and you *hate* me for it! *You wish me dead!*"

Rebecca shook her head, not at all amused by the young woman's performance. "Hate you?" she echoed. "I've pitied you," she declared truthfully. Her eyes swung first to her husband and then to Billy Starbuck. "All of you," she finished quietly. She turned to Tyree, pointedly ignoring Josiah and the look he flashed her. "What are we going to do, Simon?" she asked quietly.

Tyree was reloading the Remington, painfully aware that he probably had considerably less ammunition than Lassiter had. "That depends on what he tries next," he answered. He glanced around the small cabin, realizing just how vulnerable they were if Lassiter chose to use the dynamite.

Josiah began to speak, clearing his throat when his voice failed him. "You don't really think that he'd kill us?" he said finally. "Surely he won't deliberately slaughter five innocent people in order to take just one."

"He wants your brother," Tyree answered curtly. "He also wants the gold."

Elizabeth pushed herself away from the wall, her eyes lighting as she glimpsed a small hope for her own salvation. "Then give him what he wants," she ordered harshly. There was a long silence as the others attempted to digest her words.

Starbuck was the first to speak. "Beth," he pleaded, as if she didn't fully realize what she was saying.

The young woman tossed her head, her right eyebrow arching as she reassessed her words. "He's going to kill us," she said softly, a calculated trembling in her voice as she addressed the outlaw. Of all the people in the room, she knew that Starbuck was the most vulnerable to her charms. She gestured for him to come to her. Lowering her voice, she whispered, "The baby," cast a long, caring look at Benjamin, and then turned her eyes back on

Starbuck. "You can save us, Will," she breathed, her little-girl voice somehow sensuous as she appealed to his naive sense of honor. She took his right hand in her own. "Will?" she pleaded.

He nodded his head. Visions of a glorious and heroic death tumbled through his mind. It would be a fitting end for Billy Starbuck, he mused, giving up his life for the woman he loved—and for their child. "You'll tell him the truth about me," he asked solemnly, nodding his head at the now sleeping child, "and what I did for him?"

Elizabeth played out the outlaw's romantic fantasy. "Of course," she whispered. Aware of Josiah's eyes on her, she made sure that Starbuck remained at a proper distance.

The young outlaw pulled away from Elizabeth's grasp, unmindful of the way she held him at bay. "She's right," he said aloud, turning to face the others and pulling himself erect. "Tell Lassiter I'm coming out," he announced, looking first at Josiah and then at Tyree. "And tell him I'm bringing the gold." He started toward the strongbox.

If the outlaw's devotion to Elizabeth hadn't been so outlandishly tragic, Tyree would have laughed. Instead, he shook his head. "Not hardly," he said softly, truly sorry that Starbuck was such a fool where the young woman was concerned.

Stunned, the young outlaw halted and turned back to Tyree. "He'll let you go," he began, indignant that Tyree would interfere in his heroics. "If I give myself up, if I take him the gold . . ." Once again, he started toward the box.

"The box is empty," Tyree declared flatly. "We stashed the payroll," he continued, watching the man's face. "Lassiter and I did, at the way station at Clear Creek."

"But you said he wanted the gold!" Elizabeth argued, refusing to believe him.

Tyree nodded. "And he means to take it," he answered. Annoyed that Starbuck did not seem to understand, he explained. "Lassiter went back for the gold last night. It's in those saddlebags outside." This time, his words left no room for doubt.

"He's going to kill us," Tyree continued, his voice cold and devoid of any emotion. "All of us. Will first, if we turn him out, and then the rest of us. He can't let us go," he added, "not now."

Elizabeth stood at the door, shaking her head. "No," she murmured stubbornly. "No!"

Billy Starbuck stared at her for a long moment, still blinded by a love that had begun when he was fifteen. "We can make a deal," he said, suddenly sure of himself. "If he really wants gold, we'll offer him more than he can carry."

Tyree stared at the younger man. "Meaning what?" he demanded.

Starbuck turned and strode across the room, going directly to the buffalo robe that covered the back wall. He pulled at the right-hand corner of the thick hide, jerking it away from the wooden pegs that held it in place against the smooth logs. The robe fell away to reveal the opening to the cave. "Forty thousand," he murmured, pleased when he saw the look of astonishment on Josiah's face. "Almost every damned dime I took," he bragged, "and it's all right here."

Elizabeth was the first to recover her voice. "Forty *thousand*," she echoed, her eyes lighting. She crossed the room and peered into the darkness of the cave.

Tyree shook his head in disbelief and then felt a renewed sense of hope. The cave offered more than the treasure trove that was mesmerizing Elizabeth; it offered protection from the dynamite. And the gold would buy them time. He held out his hand to the young man. "I'll need something to show him," he said.

Starbuck nodded. Taking the lantern from the wall beside his head, he struck a match and touched it to the kerosene-soaked wick. Tyree and Josiah followed him inside.

"Show him this." The young man nodded, hefting a canvas bag clearly marked with the initials of the Santa Fe Railroad. He dropped the sack into Tyree's waiting hand.

Tyree knew from the weight of the bag that it contained a considerable amount of gold coin. "I'll need something for a white flag," he said as the men stepped back into the cabin. He stared for a time at Josiah and then shifted his eyes back to the others. Taking out his revolver, he extended it toward Starbuck. "I'm going to want this back," he said softly.

Unable to believe what he was seeing, Josiah reached out to take the weapon himself. His fingers curled around the barrel, and then withdrew as he lifted his eyes to meet Tyree's gaze.

Starbuck nodded as Tyree again offered him the weapon. "I'll give it back," he promised.

Tyree nodded. He turned and found Rebecca waiting for him. She handed him a clean square of white flannel, originally intended to be used as a diaper. The oddity of that made them both laugh. Still smiling, he shook out the cloth. "Let's hope that Lassiter has a sense of humor, too."

Rebecca reached out to touch his sleeve. "Be careful, Simon," she cautioned.

He backed away from her, letting her fingers linger on his arm, and then he was gone.

Chapter Twelve

Simon Tyree stood in front of the cabin, feeling slightly foolish as he lifted the square of white flannel above his head. He could feel himself being watched, and he instinctively knew that at this very moment he was being lined up in the sights of Kyle Lassiter's long-barreled rifle.

"The pistol, Simon!" Lassiter shouted from his hiding place among the trees. "Where's the pistol?"

Tyree dropped the bag of gold coins and let go of the flag, watching as the wind lifted the white cloth and carried it away. Keeping both hands in plain view, he opened his jacket. Lassiter, still not satisfied, called out again. "Take off the coat, Simon!"

Tyree did as he was told. Feeling the wind ripple the sweat-damp chambray at his back, he braced himself against the cold and dropped the heavy coat at his feet. "I want to talk, Kyle," he shouted, his eyes probing the undergrowth just beyond the clearing. "I want to make a trade!"

Lassiter laughed. It was a cold sound, filled with malicious humor. "You've only got one thing here that I want," he answered. "I want Starbuck." It was clear from his tone that he would not settle for anything less.

Tyree stepped away from his coat. Raising his right hand high above his head, he stooped down to pick up with his left hand the canvas bag. "This is gold, Kyle," he called out, hefting the bag as he pulled himself erect. He said nothing more, content to let Lassiter concentrate on his words and the unseen contents of the pouch.

There was another long silence and then the snapping of twigs as Lassiter moved out of the trees to the edge of the clearing. Aware that someone inside the cabin would be watching him—someone with Tyree's pistol—he was careful to stay beyond the short range of a handgun. "More tricks, Simon?" he challenged.

Tyree shook his head. He took a step forward, moving out of the shadows. "Starbuck had this hidden inside the cabin. This—" he opened the bag and spilled out the contents, scattered upon the ground "—and a lot more."

Lassiter's eyes were held by the bright glimmer of the coins that lay at Tyree's feet. "How much more?" he demanded.

Tyree fought back a smile. "More than what you've got on that horse out back," he answered truthfully.

Lassiter nodded his head and then gestured with his rifle, signaling for the driver to come forward. "We'll talk, Simon," he said finally. "About Starbuck . . . and his gold."

Billy Starbuck stared out the narrow gun port, watching as Tyree made the slow walk across the clearing to the place where Lassiter waited. He felt a sinking sensation deep in his belly as he realized how dangerous Tyree's mission was, and how critical.

"Will," Elizabeth murmured. She came up behind him, her right breast brushing his left arm as she moved to a place directly beside him, a mug of coffee in her hand. As if she were really concerned, she stared out at Tyree and at Lassiter.

"Beth," the young man breathed. He stole a sidewise glimpse at her and then returned his attention to the scene unfolding outside; his obligation to Simon Tyree was greater, at the moment, then his desire for Elizabeth. It was a feeling that was destined to be short-lived.

Elizabeth positioned herself in front of Starbuck, her back to the wall as she stared up into his face. She had been inside the cavern, had seen the sacks of gold coin hidden in a wooden crate that had become a treasure chest. The thought of the money warmed her, and she used that warmth as she spoke. "I really have missed you, Will," she said coyly, leaning against the wall in such a way that her shoulders rested squarely on the logs, her erect breasts rising and falling with each breath she took. She offered the tin of coffee to him.

Starbuck took the cup in his free hand and swallowed, a familiar warmth building deep inside his chest that did not come from the lukewarm coffee. The feeling spread to his groin, and he was unable to keep his eyes off the young woman at his side. A terrible confusion tore at him: One minute Elizabeth acted as though she couldn't stand to be near him, and the next . . .

Sensing the young man's doubt, she touched his arm, careful to keep her voice low, as if she were simply engaging him in polite conversation as she waited for him to finish his coffee. "I'm sorry for the way I've treated you, Will," she began. "And for the things I've said." Her eyelashes fluttered, as if she were fighting back tears. "It's Josiah," she sighed, making it seem that she truly was afraid of the man. "He watches me like a hawk, as if he's just waiting for me—"

"As if he's just waiting for you to make a mistake . . . to do something wrong," Starbuck interrupted. His jaw tightened. He was well acquainted with the feeling. It had been with him from the time his parents had died and Josiah had taken him into his house.

The anger Starbuck was feeling spilled over. "Why didn't you come with me, Beth?" he demanded, careful to keep his voice low, the old fears gripping him. "When I ran away from him, *why didn't you come with me?*"

Elizabeth's lower lip trembled. "The baby," she whimpered, needing an excuse. "I was going to have a baby!"

"*My* baby," Starbuck reminded her angrily. "*Mine!*"

Hiding her face against the wall, Elizabeth spun away from him. She was crying, her shoulders lifting with each muffled sob. The sight of her—the sound of her weeping—

touched the young man. He had never been able to stand to see her cry.

"Beth, don't cry. Don't." He cursed the fact that they were not alone, that Josiah was in the room with them—watching them, he realized, as he turned away from the gun port to face his elder brother.

Josiah's face was grim, his dark eyes filled with a rage that he was barely able to contain. He crossed the room, determined not to lose his temper. "What's wrong, Elizabeth?" he asked gently, knowing that Starbuck was to blame for whatever it was that had upset her.

Defensively, the outlaw answered before Elizabeth was able to compose herself. "There's nothing wrong," he replied through clenched teeth. "Not one goddamned thing!"

Enraged at his brother's blasphemy, Josiah struck out at him, but Starbuck whirled away from Josiah's hand and backed against the wall. The Remington gleamed cold and deadly in the outlaw's right hand.

"Will!" Rebecca called out, struggling to keep the panic out of her voice. She moved toward the brothers, positioning herself between them. The barrel of Starbuck's pistol was only inches from her slender waist. "Please, Will," she pleaded gently.

Elizabeth had finally composed herself. She pushed away from the wall, her hand reaching out to touch her husband's upraised arm. "Josiah, he didn't do anything," she said. She chose her next words carefully, as skillfully as a politician. "We were talking about Lassiter, about what could happen if . . ." Her voice broke, and—right on cue—the tears began again. It was all very calculated: Starbuck would think her fear made her timid, and Josiah would think that her desire for peace between the brothers kept her from telling the truth about anything rude or upsetting the outlaw might have said.

Rebecca turned to face her husband. "You heard Elizabeth," she began, feeling strange because of her new alliance with the younger woman. "Will didn't do anything." Gently, she took her husband's arm and led him away.

Elizabeth waited until Josiah and Rebecca were on the other side of the room. She inhaled deeply, the tears no longer flowing. "Take me away from him, Will," she begged. "Keep the money and take me somewhere far away from Josiah!"

The pistol Starbuck held in his right hand was suddenly very heavy. He shook his head, staring at Elizabeth's profile, uncertain as to what to do. "What about Tyree?" he said finally, nodding at the man framed by the long, narrow gun port.

Elizabeth's face hardened. "You have his gun, Will," she observed coldly.

Still unsure, Starbuck shook his head. "But *how*, Beth? *How?*" he whispered.

She moved away from him, never once looking back as she answered him. "You'll find a way, Will," she said simply. "If you really love me, you'll find a way."

He stared after her, mesmerized by the provocative movement of her hips as she walked. Of course he loved her; he had always loved her. He called out to her, at the same time swinging the pistol to point directly at his brother. "I'll find a way, Beth," he said, nodding his head.

Lassiter was still mounted on Billy Starbuck's small mare. "Forty thousand," he breathed, repeating what Tyree had just finished telling him.

The driver nodded. "He never spent the money," he said. "He hid it, like some damned make-believe outlaw."

Lassiter nodded. It was plausible when he made himself remember just who Starbuck really was. *Will Simpson*, he reminded himself, giving the once nameless stablehand his proper name. *The same kid that constantly had his nose stuck in one of those dime novels.* "And now he wants to buy his way out," he whispered, more to himself than to Tyree.

Tyree shook his head. "He wants to buy *all* of us out," he answered.

Lassiter's mind was working. He had already decided he wanted all the gold—almost as much as he wanted the outlaw. "I got to think on it," he said, enjoying the game and wanting to see Tyree squirm. "Yep!" he declared, using the rifle stock to pat the saddlebag at his right hip. "I got to think on it."

Grinning, Lassiter backed the mare away from the place where Tyree stood. He knew from the look on the driver's face that he knew about the dynamite hidden inside the saddlebag.

Tyree's fists were clenched at his sides. He watched as Lassiter retreated into the thick cover provided by the dense stand of pine. "How long, Kyle?" he shouted. Lassiter's laughter and the echoing cry of his own voice were his only answer.

Angry, Tyree turned and trudged back to the cabin. He paused only long enough to pick up his coat, not giving a damn about the sack or the gold coins that were scattered around it. The gold was only as good as what it could buy, and right now it wasn't buying him one damned thing.

He opened the door and stepped across the threshold— and found himself staring into the barrel of his own gun. "What the hell?" he demanded. Josiah and Rebecca were seated with the baby on the narrow bunk, and Elizabeth was standing at Billy Starbuck's side.

The young outlaw shrugged, and the slow grin that creased the skin at his ears was almost apologetic. "I've decided to keep the money," he said simply.

The driver cursed the outlaw and then his own stupidity. If he did nothing else, he wanted to live just long enough to make the young fool pay for every miserable moment of the last three days. "And Lassiter?" he asked, watching the boy's face. "Just what do you plan on doing about Lassiter?"

Starbuck's smile grew. "Why, hell, Simon," he began. "I'm going to let you help me take care of him!"

Tyree snorted. "Not in this lifetime."

Sure of himself, Starbuck laughed. "Sure you are. You want the horses and some help getting the coach back to the main road. I want the gold—" He paused, drawing the blond woman close "—and Elizabeth."

Tyree dreaded the next words but was powerless to stop them. His gaze shifted nervously from the outlaw to Josiah.

"And my son," Starbuck finished.

Josiah's face was one of total disbelief. He rose up off the bed, his mouth dropping open as he stared at his brother and his young wife. "Elizabeth?" he cried.

The young woman said nothing. She smiled, the truth plain in her eyes and in the arrogant toss of her head. "I love him, Josiah. I loved him long before I ever married you!"

Josiah collapsed back onto the cot. He lifted a shaky hand to his mouth, smoothing his dark beard as he struggled to comprehend what Elizabeth was saying. "Benjamin," he mumbled finally. He stared down at the recuperating child sleeping peacefully in the drawer between him and Rebecca. "No!" he said suddenly. "He's *my* son!"

There was something cruel in Billy Starbuck's sudden laughter. It was a side of the man Tyree and Rebecca had never seen, and they were both repulsed. He was enjoying himself, enjoying the pain he was inflicting on his brother.

"Do you want to know why you never had a baby, Rebecca?" the outlaw began. He laughed again, thinking of the secret he had kept all these years—innocently in the beginning, when he was too young to understand. Later, when he finally understood, he had continued to keep it quiet, partly because he wanted to spare Rebecca. He shook the thought from his mind. "A long time ago, Rebecca," he began again, "before I was ever born, Josiah was sick, *really* sick." It was strange, talking about things that he knew only from a few conversations he remembered between his parents: the whispering late at night when the house was dark and they thought him asleep. "Our sister, Caroline, was sick, too, and a baby boy they never even had a chance to name. Caroline and the baby died. And Josiah . . ." He stared at his brother. "They thought he was going to die, too," he continued, taking a deep breath. "He—"

"Shut up!" Josiah was on his feet. Forgetting the pistol, he started toward his brother, not wanting to hear the rest.

Starbuck cocked the pistol. He was remembering every quarrel, every single incident when, as a little boy, Josiah had pulled down his britches and paddled his bare butt; every damned Bible verse he had been forced to memorize, to write again and again when he made even the tiniest mistake. "He had the mumps, Rebecca. Not with the fat cheeks or the sore throat." He was thinking of his own minor bout with the disease, when he was six. "He had the other kind, with the high fever. I used to hear Pa talking about it with Mama, after you and Josiah first got married." He shook his head. "Pa used to pray to God that the disease hadn't taken Josiah's seed. . . ." It had been a long time before he understood what his father had meant.

Rebecca stared up at her husband. She rose from the bed, trying very hard to remember the gentle, laughing giant she had fallen in love with when she was sixteen. He had been so different then, before he went away to the war, and so incapable, she thought, of any deception or dishonesty. A single tear rolled down her right cheek. "How could you?" she whispered. "All these years, letting me think *I* was the one. My God, Josiah! *How could you?*" It was her inability to conceive a child that had allowed her to accept Josiah's decision to convert to a new religion and to follow the doctrine of plural marriage espoused by the Solomonites. She had loved him so much that she had been willing to do anything to give him a child—even if it meant sharing him with another woman.

"Rebecca," Josiah reached out to his wife. "It's not

true," he said, knowing inside, for the first time, that it was. Still, he could not accept it. "I never believed it was true."

Simon Tyree stood at the doorway, watching as the man's life disintegrated before his very eyes. A great surge of compassion washed through him, as much for Josiah as for Rebecca. And that was followed by an equally strong wave of contempt for the young man and woman who stood in the center of the room. When Starbuck began again, Tyree stopped him. "Shut up," he ordered softly.

"But it *is* true!" Starbuck answered belligerently.

Tyree stared into the outlaw's face, his eyes boring into the other man's until, intimidated by his harsh scrutiny, Starbuck was forced to yield. "Look at him," Tyree ordered. "Do you really think that he doesn't know?"

Starbuck turned slightly and stared across the room to where his brother stood, very much alone. A small pang of shame and guilt tore at his chest, a pain that doubled in intensity when his gaze settled on Rebecca. In his need to cause his brother pain, he had hurt her as well—perhaps even more than he had hurt Josiah. Still, he was too stubborn, too filled with rage to be repentant. "And isn't that just too damned bad," he muttered.

Tyree had moved closer to the outlaw. "You know, Will," he said softly, "if you haven't learned by now to respect your elders, then maybe it's time you learned to respect your betters." With a quickness belying his age and his size, Tyree reached out, one hand closing around the barrel of the pistol and yanking it free, the other rising and falling in a swift arc. He backhanded the younger man, the sharp sound of the single slap shattering the silence.

Tyree took one step backward, the walnut grip of the Remington feeling good against the palm of his right hand. "I've had my fill," he announced, "right up to here!" He made a quick, slashing motion at his own throat. "We've got a man out there," he said, jerking a thumb in the general direction of the unseen place outside where Kyle Lassiter was waiting, "hell-bent on leaving us in this canyon. Leaving us *dead*! Now you can stay here, wallowing in the stink of your own self-pity and your petty quarrels, or you can make up your mind you're going to live and going to get out of here! I can't do it alone!" he snapped. "I can't get all of you out of here without some help."

Starbuck stood in the center of the room rubbing his sore jaw, the salty, warm taste of blood on his tongue as he touched it against the corner of his mouth. "I'll make it on my own," he said. "Elizabeth and I. Without your help!"

Tyree laughed. "You won't make it five feet outside the front door," he reckoned. "Lassiter's got your gun and six sticks of your dynamite."

Rebecca joined Tyree at the center of the room. "What's happened to Kyle, Simon?" she asked, thinking of the man Lassiter had been. Up until now, she had admired the one-armed guard, thinking of him as someone possessed of a quiet courage.

"A profound religious experience," Tyree said dryly. "Kyle came into the world poor, and he damned near left it the same way. I think when he came out of that river, he made up his mind that his life was going to be different, that he wasn't going to have to scratch for a living anymore. He helped me hide the gold at Clear Creek, and he figured I was the only one besides him that knew it was there. With me gone . . ." He shrugged.

"And the rest of us?" Josiah asked. He crossed the floor, joining Tyree and Rebecca, still unable to look at his brother or Elizabeth.

"Excess baggage," Tyree answered honestly. "The only one he really cared about keeping alive—at least for a while—was his 'Mr. Starbuck.' "

"But to kill all of us," Rebecca whispered, still unable to understand how Lassiter could consider so great a crime.

"You can't hang more than once," Tyree reminded her.

Josiah nodded his head. "He could kill all of us, bring down the cabin, and then dig the gold out of the rubble." It was a chilling prospect, but one that made great sense from Lassiter's point of view. "He could wait a few days and then go back to Holbrook or on to Flagstaff, and tell everyone there that we had died in the river. They wouldn't even bother to look for our bodies."

"Or this cabin," Rebecca surmised. Grasping at straws, she stared into Tyree's face. "What did he say, Simon, when you told him about the gold hidden here?"

"He said he had to think about it," he answered. "He knows that he has the upper hand. What he doesn't know, is about *that*." Simon pointed to the cave beyond the back wall.

"Tyree!"

Lassiter's voice sounded from beyond the closed door, his summons jolting the sensibilities of the people within. It was as if they were afraid that he had heard their musings, and that he now knew the secret of the cabin's interior.

Tyree waved the others away from the door. This time he kept the Remington in his waistband. Opening the door just a hair, he poked his nose out and answered, "I hear you, Kyle!"

"I've made up my mind!" Lassiter shouted. There was something strange in his voice, the essence of mockery.

Tyree opened the door a bit wider and then quickly stepped back and slammed it shut. "The cave!" he roared. "Get inside the cave!"

He bolted across the room, grabbing Rebecca with one arm and scooping up the baby from the bed with the other. He raced toward the opening, Josiah, Elizabeth, and Starbuck right at his back.

The two sticks of dynamite Kyle Lassiter had lashed together and thrown landed directly in front of the cabin door. The short fuse sputtered, writhing like a crimson snake, the small flame racing toward the force that lay hidden inside the tightly packed cylinders.

A mighty roar rose up from the front of the cabin. The heavy plank door was blown off its hinges as it slammed into the interior, the entire building heaved up and out, and then it collapsed inward. A rain of cedar shingles poured in through a gaping hole where once had been the roof, a cloud of thick yellow dust rising and then settling on top of the timbers.

And then it was quiet.

Chapter Thirteen

After the blast, Simon Tyree tried to remember how he had managed to land as he had, Benjamin clutched tightly against his chest, himself flat on his back on the cold floor of the dark cavern. His spine felt compacted against his breastbone, and there was a dull ache at the back of his head. He reached back to touch the place, and when he drew his fingers away, he knew they were covered with blood.

"Simon?" Rebecca called out to him, and he felt her stir. She was on his right side, beneath his arm, and sounding as though she was in a great deal of pain. "The baby, Simon . . ."

Afraid of what he might find, Tyree rubbed Benjamin's small back, his fingers making a slow circle between the child's shoulders. He was relieved to feel the even up and down rise of the boy's rib cage, amazed that he had survived the blast without any apparent injury and without crying out. "Well, trooper," he whispered to the boy, "it's a hell of a way to make a living, isn't it?" He felt Benjamin's fingers wind around his thumb. "He's all right, Rebecca," he said.

Gradually, the others began to come to their senses. There was the muted sound of coughing as Elizabeth tried to clear the dust from her lungs, and then the quiet noise of her angry whispers as she argued with Starbuck. Then

144

Josiah stirred, inhaling sharply as he rose up on one knee, a soft whistle coming from between his compressed lips as he felt a ragged cut just below his kneecap.

Tyree rose up on one elbow, concerned about Rebecca. She was quiet—much too quiet. He called out to her again. "Rebecca?"

There was a brief silence before she whispered, "I'm all right, Simon." It took her a little time, but she was finally able to sit up, her whole body feeling battered and bruised. She groped in the darkness, listening for the sound of Tyree's breathing, her ears straining for the lighter noise of the baby's breath, feeling whole only when the child was in her arms, his small head pressed comfortably against her breast. "Thank God," she breathed.

Relieved of his small burden, Tyree sat up. He dug into his shirt pocket and searched for his metal matchbox, relieved when his numb fingers closed around the brass cylinder. "Will," he called out softly.

The sound of loose gravel and broken glass preceded the young man's answer. "Over here." The subtle smell of kerosene drifted on the still air as Starbuck righted the overturned lantern. "You have any matches?" he asked.

"In a minute," Tyree answered, and then called out softly, "Josiah?" He already knew that Elizabeth was all right. Her whispered complaints were unnaturally loud in the cryptlike stillness.

"Here," Josiah answered. There was the rustle of cloth as he stirred.

Tyree silently assessed their situation, wishing that his eyes would adjust to the eerie darkness. Other than the noise of their measured breathing, there was only silence. No sound reached out to them from beyond the blackness, and there was absolutely no light.

It was the absence of light that concerned Tyree most. Struggling to keep his voice calm, he spoke again to the younger man. "Will, bring me the lantern."

Starbuck stayed on his knees, feeling his way along the floor of the cavern. He followed the sound of Tyree's voice until his groping fingers touched the smooth leather of the driver's right boot, then he reached up until their hands met. Tyree took the lantern and, not wanting to waste a match to locate the wick, searched for it with his fingers. Feeling the wetness of the coarse cotton and then the oily metal of the lamp's base, he decided to set the lantern on the floor before lighting it.

The pungent scent of sulphur and kerosene blended, the wick flaring a bright yellow against the black emptiness at the rear of the cavern. One by one, the pale faces appeared in the soft glow, heads without bodies that seemed to hover in the darkness.

Rebecca was the first to speak, her voice filled with alarm as she reached out to touch Tyree's neck. "My God, Simon," she murmured, unable to hide her concern. The blood from his head wound trickled down from behind his ear, warm against her fingers, and disappeared beneath his collar.

He reached up, his hand closing around her fingers. "I'm all right," he lied.

They all lapsed into a grim silence again. Even the baby was subdued, his blue eyes wide as he stared at the lantern. They were locked in their private thoughts, their minds trying to grasp what had happened, their eyes busily searching the dark corners for some way out.

"It's like being buried alive," Starbuck finally whispered, his voice betraying the thin edge of control that was dangerously close to breaking. He could feel the walls of the cavern closing in on him, and it was difficult for him to breathe. The soft light of the lantern washed across his face, smoothing the faint lines that had begun to mark his features, making him appear as young and innocent as Benjamin.

Tyree forced himself to speak again, refusing to give in to the melancholy that was threatening to possess him. "How far back does this cave go?" he asked.

Starbuck thought before he answered. "There's another passage, farther back," he said, gesturing with his head. "I don't know where it goes, or how far," he confessed. "I never had the time to look."

Tyree nodded. He had the feeling that fear had in fact prevented the outlaw from exploring the depths of the cave. He had noticed during his initial visit into the cavern, when Starbuck had showed him the chest containing the money, that almost all of the young man's belongings were grouped at the very front. "What else have you got in here," he asked, "besides the money?"

"Some salt pork," Starbuck answered. "Water and grain for the mare. Not much else." He shrugged. And then he reconsidered. "Some tools. They were already here when I found the cabin. Shovels, a pickax, a pry bar . . . and a broad ax," he finished.

Josiah spoke up. "We can dig out," he said hopefully.

"We can try," Tyree agreed.

"And Lassiter?" Elizabeth's voice rose, her tone filled with a scathing ridicule. "If we manage to dig ourselves out, what will we do about Lassiter?"

Tyree grimaced, his eyes on the young woman's face. "I'll deal with Lassiter when the time comes," he growled. *Just like I'll deal with you and Starbuck,* he thought silently.

Elizabeth's right eyebrow arched, as if she had read Tyree's thoughts. Her steady gaze locked on the man's face. She started to speak and then changed her mind, a benign smile appearing as she eased back down on her haunches and into the open arms of Billy Starbuck. This time, she was holding on to him. "Whatever you say, Mr. Tyree," she said softly, her fingers laced in Starbuck's hair.

After calming the spooked horses and making sure they were uninjured, Kyle Lassiter stood in the rubble of the destroyed cabin, his face betraying confusion. He wiped his chin, one eye narrowing as he peered beneath the torn and brittle timbers for some sign of life. *Death,* he thought, correcting himself.

There was nothing—not even beneath the remains of the large ponderosa pine that had been uprooted and had crashed down across the back wall of the small cabin.

Perplexed, Lassiter dusted off the remains of the small bed and sat down on one corner.

He was facing the downed pine tree. The heavy limbs of the ancient evergreen obscured almost the entire back wall of the cabin; a portion of the roof had collapsed beneath the thick limbs. Lassiter stared at the tree, something gnawing at the back of his mind. It was the back wall—the unexplained sturdiness of the back wall.

He stood up and took a step backward. It was, he supposed, possible for Tyree and the others to be buried beneath the pine tree and the portion of the peaked roof that was leaning against the wall . . .

He shook his head. "No," he breathed, his eyes drifting to the other three walls of the cabin. The force of the blast had lifted the individual logs from their bracings, scattering them like so many matchsticks. They lay a considerable distance from the cabin's stone foundation, torn and split as much by the effect of the explosion as by their abrupt flight and harsh landing against the rocky earth.

Again Lassiter's eyes swung to the sturdy back wall. The timbers remained almost exactly in the original fittings, piled one atop the other, only a slight backward lean in their upward stack. *As if,* Lassiter realized, *they are resting against something for support.* . . .

Instantly, his gaze shot upward. A sheer, sandstone cliff rose up before him, the faint outline of the upper portion of the cabin a brighter yellow against the naked rock where the roof had once rested flush against the face of the cliff.

Elated, Lassiter did a one-man jig. *A cave!* he rejoiced. *The back wall of the cabin must have concealed the entrance to a mine shaft!* It was a fitting hiding place for Billy Starbuck's treasure.

But if there was a cave, there was also a good possibility that Tyree and the others had survived, that they, as well as the money, were hidden behind the remains of the roof and the heavy pine.

The man's laughter was sardonic. His dreams of a

fortune were fast fading before a grim reality. He was a one-armed man, standing amidst litter that a half-dozen fit men would have difficulty removing, litter separating him from untold wealth.

He was not, he decided, destined to die a poor man, not with the money he had retrieved from the stove pipe at the Clear Creek way station and Billy Starbuck's stash of another forty thousand only a few feet away. He knew he could ride away right now and live fairly well on the money he already had, but so little stood in the way of him and enough money to set himself up as a rich man for life. Furthermore, if he left Tyree and the others behind, they might survive—and he would always have to look over his shoulder. But if he made sure they were dead—and took Starbuck's gold in the process—it would be assumed that they perished in the sudden flood. As for the dead man at Clear Creek, Billy Starbuck would be given the blame.

Resigned to what he must do, Lassiter sighed and stretched. He took his time, knowing that there was no need for urgency. And then, gingerly, he picked his way through the rubble on the cabin floor, looking for an opening among the pine boughs that would grant him entrance to the darkness behind the downed portion of the cabin's roof. "Tyree," he called, his voice raising. "*Simon Tyree!*"

Tyree jumped, the sound of Lassiter's voice jarring his senses and making him instantly alert. He pressed a finger to his lips, signaling for the others to remain silent.

Lassiter called out to him again, his voice sounding surprisingly close. Tyree could hear the noise of dry lumber being torn away from wooden pegs and bracings, and then the sound of the man's muffled swearing.

"He knows we're here," Starbuck said, his voice a strange mixture of apprehension and relief.

"He knows the gold is here," Tyree snorted. He rubbed his hands together, fighting the numbness that radiated from the back of his head to the ends of his fingers.

Josiah crawled closer. "What are we going to do, Tyree?" The tender exchanges between Rebecca and Tyree had not escaped him, and the memory put an edge to his words.

Benjamin started to whimper, the anxiety of the adults finally beginning to affect him. His whines gave way to a lusty howl.

"Shut up!" Elizabeth blurted as she moved toward Rebecca. She raised her hand, slapping out at the infant's chubby cheek. "*Shut up!*"

Rebecca grabbed the younger woman's arm. "Don't touch him, Elizabeth," she rasped. "Don't you *dare* touch him!" She rose up on her knees and spun away from the younger woman. "Simon," she said calmly, soothing the infant with her hands. "Lassiter does know that we're here."

Tyree nodded, curtly. "He knows."

"But he doesn't know how many of us are alive," she reasoned. She reached out, touching his shoulder, her fingers sliding down his arm as she gently guided their joined hands to the pistol in his waistband.

The darkness hid Tyree's smile. "Answer him, Rebecca," he said softly, understanding what she was suggesting and appreciating her wisdom. "The next time he calls out for me, answer him."

Rebecca nodded, and when Lassiter repeated the driver's name, she made her reply. "Simon's dead, Mr. Lassiter," she answered, her voice flat and devoid of any emotion. There was only a fleeting feeling of guilt over the small but necessary deception.

There was a brief silence, and then the sound of labor resumed as Lassiter pulled and tugged at the wooden planking that had once formed the roof of the small building. "How many?" he demanded.

Rebecca took a deep breath. "Simon's dead," she repeated. "Josiah's leg is hurt, but Elizabeth and the baby are all right." She paused, instinctively knowing that Lassiter would not believe her if she said that the outlaw was dead, too. She also sensed that Lassiter needed more than the gold to inspire his efforts, and a live Billy Starbuck would fill that need. "Will is fine."

Lassiter seemed satisfied with her answer. "I'll need help," he said, continuing to work.

Tyree was already whispering instructions to the other two men. He ordered Starbuck to locate the tools, and when they had been found, he passed the small shovel to Josiah, grabbing the pry bar for himself. "He's going to try to make a deal," he whispered into Rebecca's ear. "The crate of gold for your freedom."

Starbuck was already scraping at the base of the collapsed roof with his shovel, grunting from the effort. "And if we give it to him?" he asked, mentally marking off the place he would start digging away at the pile of smashed rock.

"He's still got dynamite," Tyree observed. "You put the strongbox out before *you* get out, and he'll seal up the cave. And this time, he'll make damned sure that we all die."

"Then we don't give him the box," Starbuck said grimly.

They continued to work, Lassiter on one side of the collapsed wall, Tyree and the rest on the other. Finally Lassiter paused, pounding on the few planks that remained between them. "There's a tree down," he called. "I want to leave the frame of the roof in place and let it support the tree until you get out!" He beat against the smooth one-by-sixes with his fist. "Knock out this board first," he shouted. "And then the two beside it."

Starbuck and Tyree looked at each other, stifling laughter. The opening Lassiter had crudely outlined with his thumps was just about the size of a small crate. Tyree reached up, signaling for Starbuck to move in closer with the sputtering lantern. With his fingers, he tapped at two more planks at the outer edge of Lassiter's small square. "If he's telling the truth about the tree, there'll still be enough support from these to form a decent brace."

Starbuck moved to a place beside his brother, and together the two of them beat at the dried planking.

Tyree turned his back on the brothers. Grimly, with Rebecca's help, he pushed and shoved the crate of gold into the far reaches of the dark cavern. Elizabeth, her arms folded across her chest, watched them, making no effort to help. She answered Tyree's look of contempt with the same benign smile she had exhibited earlier.

A faint glow of light broke through the small opening Starbuck had battered in the top of the yellow planking. Dirt and wood dust danced on the silver beam, the stream of bright luminescence suddenly blinding the occupants of the dark cavern. They withdrew from the light momentarily and then resumed their chores.

Tyree moved quickly to the front of the cavern, pulled the Remington from his waistband, and shoved it into the top of his boot. Pulling his pant leg over the weapon, he fell face forward, positioning himself on the floor, his arms well above his head.

Starbuck prepared himself for a final attack on the wooden plank before him. He raised his arms, the heavy ax above his head as he prepared to strike. But he stopped midswing, when the very tip of the barrel of Lassiter's rifle poked through the opening.

"Back off, boy." Lassiter's face appeared in the opening.

The weight of the heavy ax and its awkward, upraised position caused a wave of intense pain to shoot through Starbuck's shoulders and neck. The temptation to complete the downward arc, to bury the blade of the ax in Lassiter's face, was almost more than he could bear. He tensed, the tendons in his neck knotting as he considered his chances.

Lassiter grinned down at the man and moved the rifle against Starbuck's nose. "Go ahead and swing," he coaxed, thumbing back the hammer on the rifle. Carefully, Starbuck lowered the ax and laid it on the floor. Then he backed away. Lassiter, smiling his approval, poked his head inside the opening, staring for a time at the prone form of Simon

Tyree, nodding his head in satisfaction and then withdrawing. "And now for the money." He sneered.

Rebecca joined Starbuck, her free hand on his shoulder. When the wind from the outside reached her, she was almost sorry to lose the warmth of the snug cavern. "Not yet, Mr. Lassiter," she answered. Taking her hand from Starbuck's shoulder, she reached out of the small opening, clearly expecting Lassiter's assistance.

Completely taken aback, Lassiter withdrew slightly. Then propping the rifle between his hip and his elbow, he offered the woman his hand.

Rebecca stepped through the small hole with Benjamin pressed firmly against her breast. She smiled a cool thank-you to the man and then stood back. "Elizabeth," she called softly.

Shading her eyes, Elizabeth clambered through the opening, ducked under the heavy branches of the fallen evergreen, and made her way outside the demolished cabin. Josiah and Starbuck followed after her.

Rebecca turned to Lassiter and answered the question before he could ask it. "The crate is at the back of the cave, Mr. Lassiter." She carefully avoided looking at his single arm as she continued. "And it's too heavy and too badly damaged for you or the others to lift through that hole."

Lassiter's eyes narrowed. "Then we'll just have to figure another way to get it out, won't we? One bag at a time," he said softly.

Elizabeth stared at the man, her eyes crawling across him, head to toe, as she made a slow appraisal. He returned her silent scrutiny, and she felt certain that his lingering, hungry gaze was a good sign; he was ripe for her to manipulate.

Lassiter had a gun and, clearly, the upper hand. The gold inside the cavern was his, unless . . . Then she remembered Tyree, feigning death, and realized what would happen if he succeeded in killing Lassiter: Tyree would control the money, just as he would inevitably control and contain Billy Starbuck.

She made her decision and stepped up to Lassiter, her words coming in a soft whisper. "Tyree's not dead."

Lassiter's head snapped up, tilting at an uncanny angle as he studied the young woman's face. "What?"

Elizabeth tossed her head, her blond curls dancing across her forehead as she placed her hands on her hips. "Tyree is still alive," she said again, smiling at the man. When she saw that he believed, she continued, sashaying forward, a premeditated back and forth movement in her hips. The farm-girl innocence, the whining demeanor, was gone. She reached out to caress Lassiter's cheek. "He has a gun," she murmured, "and he means to use it."

"Beth!" Starbuck said, not believing what he was hearing. He started toward her, stopping in his tracks when Lassiter swung the barrel of the rifle in his direction.

Josiah said nothing, and Rebecca simply shook her head; nothing Elizabeth had done or could do surprised her.

Without looking at the young woman who stood before him, Lassiter called out to Tyree. "I know you're alive, Simon," he roared. "Goddamn you! *I know!*" Enraged, he turned back to the cave. With a slow, deadly purpose, he fired into the opening. The heavy lead slug tore through the darkness, the screaming whine and ping of the ricochets echoing for what seemed an eternity.

Tyree compacted himself against the cold floor of the cavern, his arms instinctively going over his head as he protected his face and ears from the coarse bits of rock that sliced through the air to tear into his flesh and clothing. *Elizabeth*, he thought bitterly. *It must have been Elizabeth*.

The sound of the shot died and faded into infinity. There was a long, tense silence, and then Lassiter called out again. "I want the pistol, Simon! And then I want you!"

Tyree knew it was useless, but a spark of hope remained. He fished into his boot, drawing the Remington, praying for one clear shot. And then, drawing himself up onto his knees, he made his way to the opening and stared out into the light.

Lassiter was standing in the open, on the front porch. Elizabeth was beside him, and in front of him . . .

Rebecca. Lassiter had placed Rebecca and Benjamin directly in front of himself—directly in the line of fire.

Uncocking the Remington, Tyree resignedly reached his hand through the opening, the pistol dangling harmlessly from his outstretched fingers. He dropped it on the scarred remains of the cabin floor, calling out, "There's the gun, Kyle."

Lassiter pushed Rebecca away and stepped across the threshold. Aiming for the gaping hole in the side wall, Lassiter kicked the weapon across the floor. The pistol spun in a series of tight circles and came to rest in a dark corner in a pile of debris.

Lassiter stood just outside the entrance to the cavern. "Come on out, Simon," he cajoled, waiting.

Tyree stepped through the opening, bending forward as he lowered his head and ducked through the rough planking of the downed roof.

There was a swift whisper of air beside Tyree's head as Lassiter brought the barrel of his rifle up and then down, slamming into the driver's neck. The force of the blow carried Tyree forward, reopening the wound at the base of his skull as he sprawled, belly down, across the rough floor. A gush of bright, red blood spattered the planking beside his head, the dry wood greedily soaking up the wetness.

Chapter Fourteen

It took a long time for Josiah Simpson and Billy Starbuck to remove the cache of stolen gold from the interior of the dark cave. They worked in total silence, each of them feeling powerless to stop whatever it was that Kyle Lassiter had planned for them.

They were retrieving the final sacks of gold when Starbuck bent down and picked up the ax he had used to hack their way out of the cavern. It was the only weapon available to him, but its size made it virtually impossible to conceal. He examined it, turning it over and over in his hands as he pondered a way to get it out of the cavern undetected.

Sensing his brother's intentions, Josiah reached out, taking hold of the tool. "Don't be a fool!" he whispered. "Lassiter's sure to see, and then where will we be?"

Starbuck laughed, the soft sound laced with the sardonic contempt he had always felt for his elder brother. He wrenched the tool away from Josiah and without another word sat down on the hard ground, intent on working the handle of the ax up the inside of his pant leg. The store-tailored trousers were tight—too tight to hide entirely the long-handled ax—but still he tried. "You saw what he did to Tyree, Josiah," he said softly. "If we don't do something to stop him, he's going to kill us all."

Stubbornly, Josiah shook his head. "No," he said.

156

"Lassiter's not that desperate. He has the money and the horses. He'll just leave us here, and we'll be all right. There's food and water, and in time, someone will come."

If, he thought, *you don't cause any trouble, little brother.*

"I won't let you do this, Will," he said solemnly. His fingers closed around Starbuck's wrist, and this time he held on.

But Starbuck refused to yield. A hundred times, when he was growing up, he had heard the stories of how his older brother had gone willingly off to war and had come home with a chest full of medals. Josiah himself had boasted about what he had done—about how important it was that a man "did his duty," how necessary it was to serve and to honor his country, his cause . . .

His god.

"Onward, Christian soldiers," Starbuck murmured disgustedly, thinking of the hymn the Solomonites sang almost every Sunday. The majority of them were war veterans, too; they gloried in their old war and then turned the other cheek when there was trouble or when they were told to move on, just like Josiah was doing now.

No matter how hard Starbuck tried, the ax would not fit into his pant leg. Angry, he dropped it into the dirt, his fingers still laced around the shaft. "You're going to have to help, Josiah," he said finally, trying hard not to lose his temper or to sound disrespectful. Then he gave up, unable to continue the charade. *"Goddammit! You've got to help!"* he whispered. Resolutely, he shoved the ax into his brother's hand.

"Lassiter will let us go!" Josiah argued.

Starbuck snorted in disgust. "Tyree could be dead," he began, feeling a sense of genuine remorse as he said the words. "For Christ's sake, Josiah, you've got to help, if not for yourself, then for Rebecca and Elizabeth—*and for the baby!*" He realized as soon as he said the words that he had made a mistake.

Josiah's jaw tightened, his face suddenly hard and

devoid of color. For a brief, frightening moment, he remained silent, and then he took the ax.

If nothing else, he was going to live long enough to see Elizabeth and his brother punished for their transgressions. In his bitterness, he never even considered Rebecca or the child.

From outside, Lassiter called out to the two men, his words cutting into the tense silence between them. When they did not immediately answer, he cocked the rifle. "I want you out here *now!*" he roared. He fired once, the loud report of the rifle thundering down the length of the shallow canyon.

Quickly, Starbuck dropped down to one knee beside his brother's leg, the ax in his hand. Josiah's homespun trousers were loose fitting and a bit long, but with a degree of caution and a minor diversion, there was a chance—a slim chance—that he could conceal the ax and carry it outside.

Starbuck untucked his shirt, tearing off a narrow strip from the tail and using it to secure the blade end of the ax to Josiah's ankle. "Lassiter's seen you limping," he said quietly, without looking at his brother, arranging the man's pant cuff. "Stay behind me, and act like the leg's giving you trouble."

"I'll do what I have to do," Josiah said curtly, his words filled with a strange foreboding.

Starbuck left the cavern first. He hesitated at the door, reaching back to grab the last bag, which Josiah hefted through the opening. He was careful to position himself in such a way that when Josiah put his stiff leg through the hole Lassiter would not see anything strange or out of the ordinary.

"That the last of it?" Lassiter asked, his eyes on the bags and nothing else.

Starbuck nodded. "That's it." He moved forward, two bags of gold he had carried from the cavern in his hands. "Let the women go, Lassiter," he began. And then, on purpose, he dropped one of the sacks. The heavy gold coins ruptured the seam and spilled out onto the floor.

Lassiter jumped back as if he had been stung. "You goddamn fool!" There was a desperation in him as the coins rolled across the wood in a dozen different directions. Elizabeth dropped to her knees, scurrying after the coins, but she didn't seem to move fast enough. "Pick it up," Lassiter ordered, shoving the barrel of his rifle into Starbuck's flat belly. "Now!"

Obediently, Starbuck did as he was told. On his hands and knees, he crawled after the coins, Elizabeth just ahead of him. When he attempted to retrieve a pair of gold eagles, she slapped his hand away. "No!" she breathed. He watched as she worshiped the coins with her fingers and at last understood what she had been feeling.

It was the money! She wasn't mad at him; she was just afraid that they would lose their money. "Beth," he whispered.

She shook her head, still in pursuit of the other coins that lay scattered on the floor. She hurried after them, turning around to move back toward the place where Josiah stood.

Josiah was behind Lassiter. He had bent down, his right leg strangely extended in front of him, straight and unbending. Quickly, he struggled to untie the thin strip of cloth Starbuck had tied around his boot.

Intending to order him out of her way, Elizabeth paused in her pursuit of the gold and stared up into her husband's face. The cold in his eyes—the silent, utter contempt—chilled her, stopping her dead in her tracks. She retreated, resting on her heels, the words frozen in her throat.

And then she saw the ax. Fearing more for her own safety than for Lassiter's, she screamed.

Lassiter spun around, the rifle making a great arc as he faced Josiah. He saw the flash of sun on the blade of the ax before he saw anything else. "You bastard," he hissed. He backed away, motioning with the rifle. "Lay it down," he ordered, watching as the long-handled ax slid out from Josiah's pant leg. "Now back up."

For a long time, Lassiter simply stared at the ax. And then, his eyes lighting, he turned his gaze on Starbuck.

The young outlaw rose up from the floor, his eyes never leaving Lassiter's face. He cleared his throat, unable to read anything in the man's seemingly benign countenance. "You've got the gold, Lassiter," he began. He held out the handful of coins he had picked up from the porch floor. "You can let the women go. You can let us all go."

Lassiter snorted. He smiled and pointed to where Elizabeth was again busy picking up coins. "*She* isn't going anywhere," he said. "At least, not with you!"

Starbuck's face turned bright red. "She'll go," he said brashly and then pointed at the sacks of gold at Lassiter's feet. "It only took me six months to make that. I can make it again."

"And you think she'll wait?" Lassiter was in no particular hurry now. He had the gold and the horses that were still tethered beyond the cabin; he could afford to take some time. He called out to the young woman, "You going to go with him, little girl?" His voice was deceptively soft, honeyed. He already knew the answer but wanted to hear her say the words. "You going to wait for him to rebuild his fortune?" It amused him that the young hellion could be so stupid where the slut was concerned.

Elizabeth turned around. Slowly she stood up, the front of her dress now a makeshift apron filled with the bright glimmer of gold, one hand securing the fortune she had recovered from the floor. "I'm going with *you*," she said, tossing her head, not doubting for a moment that he intended to take her.

Billy Starbuck turned around. "Beth . . ."

Moving away from the outlaw and going toward Lassiter, the young woman laughed. It was a harsh sound, full of nothing but cold ridicule. "For God's sake, Will!"

"You loved me!" he argued. "You had my baby!"

She spun around, facing him. "You were a way out. Nothing more than a way to get free of Josiah and my father!" Elizabeth felt anew the old anger she had felt when Starbuck had run away without her. She raised her head arrogantly. "As for the baby, you never took proper time to make a baby. Hello, good-bye," she hissed, mocking him for his frantic, hurried lovemaking. "There was Josiah at night, on his knees praying for . . ." Her eyes turned on the elder Simpson. "For the *strength* to make one, and you . . ."

There was something inherently wicked in Elizabeth, a genuine need to hurt and mock any man who touched her, who found her attractive. "I have no idea who the baby's father is," she continued. "But I do know this. Neither you nor your brother were man enough to make him!"

Dumbfounded, Billy Starbuck stared at the young woman. "I . . ."

Lassiter was laughing. "Well, now," he grinned. He turned his eyes to Elizabeth. "And you want to go with me," he said.

She flounced over to the man, her fingers raking his hair. The money in her skirt was still clenched against her heart. "I *am* going with you!" she announced.

Roughly, Lassiter shoved her away, and she stumbled backward, the gold coins that were in her skirt spilling and scattering around and away from her. He stared down at her. "I bought women like you for a dollar a throw in Holbrook," he mocked. "In Mexico I paid even less."

Elizabeth sprang to her feet, and like a wounded wildcat, she charged Lassiter, screaming, both arms raised above her head. The thought of the man leaving her with Josiah and Will—of taking the money and going away— filled her with a great rage and an even greater fear. "You bastard!" she screeched. "You sniveling, one-armed cripple!"

Dispassionately, Lassiter raised the rifle and fired. The bullet tore into Elizabeth's chest, penetrating the softness beneath her right breast. She staggered, the impact of the bullet carrying her back a full yard. Her fingers went to the small hole in her dress, and when she lifted them away they were bright red with blood. "No . . ." she begged. "*No-o-o-o*. . . ." She fell to the floor at Rebecca's feet, dead.

Stunned, Josiah and Starbuck stood frozen until the sound of Lassiter recocking the rifle brought them back to their senses.

Immediately, Lassiter leveled the weapon at the brothers. "She had it coming," he rasped, her final words still ringing in his ears: . . . *sniveling, one-armed cripple!*

Lassiter jabbed the rifle at Josiah's stomach. "You, over here." He motioned to a place near the front door of the cabin. "You, too," he said to Rebecca. He waited until she was with Josiah before he spoke again.

Starbuck stood in the center of the group, feeling totally naked and vulnerable. He swallowed, his mouth suddenly dry and his throat tight.

Lassiter positioned himself so that he could see the three of them. His eyes flicked from one face to the other, finally settling on Starbuck. He pointed the cocked rifle at the young man's belt buckle, grinning coldly when he sucked in his belly.

"You know what you cost me when you did this?" he asked quietly, shrugging his shoulder, using muscles that had been long neglected as he raised all that remained of his left arm. The stub convulsed like a grotesque flipper. Lassiter continued, his voice strangely calm and deceptively soft. "You cost me my job. Twenty years with the railroad, and it was all gone." Lassiter purposely chose to ignore the fact that the railroad had offered him a desk job in their Chicago office, a position that he still considered demeaning and without honor. "My *job,* man!" he said again. This time his voice broke, betraying the rage that lay just beneath the veneer of his sanity.

Carefully, Rebecca took a single step forward. "Let us go, Mr. Lassiter." She hated to beg, but she couldn't bear to think of anything happening to Benjamin—or to the others. *"Please."*

Lassiter grinned. "Oh, I'm going to let *you* go, Mrs. Simpson," he lied. "You and the baby." His smile grew. "Maybe even your man."

Rebecca inhaled, her bottom lip drawn in between her front teeth. "And Will?" she asked weakly.

Lassiter's smile faded. He backed away from the woman, swinging the rifle in the direction of a tangled mass of leather that lay on the ground. "I want him tied," he whispered. "There!" Again the tip of the rifle barrel indicated the place.

Puzzled, Josiah hesitated. "I . . ."

"*There!*" Lassiter interrupted harshly. He nodded at two side posts that still remained standing. When Josiah failed to respond, Lassiter aimed at a spot between the man's feet and fired, the bullet plowing a deep furrow in the wood, a ridge forming as it tore through the plank beneath Josiah's left foot. Immediately, Lassiter levered the rifle, feeding another cartridge into the chamber. He turned his attention on Billy Starbuck. "Get down there," he barked.

The young man did as he was told, dropping down to his knees.

Josiah felt helpless as Lassiter turned quickly around and again pointed the rifle at him. "For God's sake, Lassiter," said Josiah, "you can't do this!"

"Tie one arm to each post," Lassiter rasped, ignoring the man's plea. He poked the barrel of the rifle into the soft flesh at the base of the kneeling Starbuck's skull. "Do it, Simpson, or so help me God, I'll blow his brains out right now!"

"Do it, Josiah!" Starbuck shouted. The unknown, he felt, was better than Lassiter simply spattering his brains across the landscape.

Josiah did as he was told, using leather straps to secure his brother's wrists close to the ground on each post. Perhaps, he thought piously, all Lassiter had in mind was a thrashing. It would be humiliating for his brother, but well deserved, and it was better than dying. He finished his chore and stepped away.

Lassiter surveyed Josiah's handiwork. Satisfied, he nodded his head. "The ax," he said quietly. "Get me the ax."

Rebecca bolted forward, Benjamin perched on her right hip. "You can't be serious!" she declared, standing in front of Starbuck. She felt Josiah at her shoulder, angry with him when he forcibly restrained and pulled her away.

Lassiter only smiled. "You ought to understand why I'm doing this, Josiah," he said matter-of-factly, "you being a man ordained to teach and evangelize for the Solomonites. An eye for an eye," he intoned. "An arm for an arm." The last words came through clenched teeth. "I want the ax!" he repeated.

Josiah shook his head, refusing the man's order. Coming from Lassiter's mouth, the sacred words seemed more blasphemous than had Starbuck's impassioned cursings.

Using the rifle as a prod, Lassiter pushed Josiah and Rebecca aside and sprinted up the two steps leading to the porch. Awkwardly he picked up the ax while retaining his hold on the rifle.

He stepped back down into the dirt beside the porch, both weapons in his arm. Lifting the rifle slightly, he propped the weapon up against the foundation of the cabin, making sure that he was standing between it and the others. His fingers closing around the long handle of the ax, he addressed Josiah and Rebecca, his voice a flat monotone. "I mean to take his arm," he said firmly. "You interfere, I could miss." It was a thinly veiled threat, meant as much for husband and wife as for the outlaw. Satisfied that they would not interfere, he raised the ax.

Tyree was conscious, as he had been for some time. He was aware of the voices that seemed to echo inside his head, and a terrible pain was eating at the base of his skull.

He could see the strange episode that was unfolding between Starbuck and Lassiter with startling clarity and instantly comprehended the horror of what was now happening. A surge of anger flooded through him as he looked at a subdued and impotent Josiah Simpson. The man was doing nothing; he was content, it seemed, to wallow in his role of passive observer, not giving a damn about his brother—or his wife and the child.

Cautiously, Tyree raised his head, fighting the nausea that clawed at his belly, and rested his chin on his forearm. Lassiter's back was to him, the ax in the man's hand raised high above his head, where it remained poised, motionless.

Reaching out, Tyree groped in the shadows at the tip of his fingers. He could see the blue-gray gleam of the Remington's barrel just beyond his reach. Inch by inch, he pulled himself to the weapon and picked it up, and then silently began to lift himself to his knees.

Rebecca screamed, and Tyree saw the downward flash of steel as the ax arced toward the earth with great force. There was a second scream, this time the terrified yelp of Billy Starbuck . . . and then silence.

Lassiter began to laugh. "Practice swing," he said loudly. The ax blade was buried in the wood only inches from Starbuck's left ear. Lassiter worked the blade back and forth in an effort to pull it free. "This time," he promised, whispering the words in Starbuck's ear, "it's for real." He raised the ax again.

Rebecca tore away from Josiah, but he reached out and pulled her back, struggling to hold her in place. Abruptly, she stopped fighting and faced him. "Do something, Josiah!" If nothing else, she wished he would take Benjamin from her and free her to do what he would not. She held the infant out to the man, pleading with him. *"Please!"*

Josiah backed away from her, his head slowly rocking side to side, rejecting the child. He turned to Lassiter and whispered, "Let him go." Half-heartedly, he reached out to grab the man's arm.

Lassiter stopped midswing, pivoting to avoid Josiah's grasping fingers. His face contorted, betraying the rage he felt at being interrupted in his perverse game with Billy Starbuck. He raised the ax again, this time aiming the blade at Josiah's pale forehead.

Tyree was on his feet. Carefully, with the palm of his left hand, he muffled the sound as he cocked the Remington, aware of Rebecca's gaze as he aimed the pistol. She remained in place, remarkably calm, no emotion showing in her face to betray him, relief flooding her emerald eyes.

And then her expression changed, a poignant sadness replacing the relief as Tyree hesitated. She seemed to understand what was going through his mind—the temptation to let Lassiter free her of Josiah. Unable to meet her eyes, Tyree turned his gaze from her and the baby she held in her arms, his whole being seeming to harden.

Josiah saw Tyree, too, and he stared up at the man, already grateful for his certain salvation. The feeling of gratitude quickly ebbed as he looked into Tyree's pale eyes. He was aware, suddenly, of the man's contemptuous appraisal, sensing something in Tyree's eyes that was more frightening than the madness he had observed in Lassiter's. He closed his eyes, sure that Lassiter was going to kill him—and that Tyree was going to do nothing to stop him.

Tyree made his decision reluctantly. It would be so easy, he mused, to allow Lassiter to complete his swing and to let Josiah Simpson die. He pushed the dark thought from his mind, remembering instead what he had seen in Rebecca's eyes. And then, his voice barely above a whisper, he called out, "Kyle." When the one-armed man froze, he repeated the word louder. "Kyle!"

Lassiter turned around, the ax still poised above his head. His face was only inches from the barrel of Tyree's gun, and he lifted his eyes to meet Tyree's cold scrutiny. For a moment, no one breathed.

Point-blank, Tyree fired, watching as the ax slipped from Lassiter's dead fingers. This time Tyree had not hesitated, and there was not one mote of regret or forgiveness in his blue-gray eyes.

Tyree dropped down to the ground beside Starbuck. He holstered his pistol, his head aching fiercely as he bent forward to untie the leather thongs that bound the outlaw's wrists. "A little late in your life for prayer, isn't it, Starbuck?" he asked, helping the man up off his knees.

Gamely, Starbuck forced a broad smile. "It worked, didn't it?" He flexed both arms, purposely not looking at the body that lay at his feet.

Rebecca slowly came forward, Benjamin still clutched in one arm. She hesitated, but then wrapped her other arm around the younger man. They held each other for a long time, Benjamin between them, and they needed no words to express what they were feeling. When she pulled away, Tyree could see she had been crying.

Josiah stared at the carnage at Tyree's feet. The back of Lassiter's head was completely blown away. In spite of all the things the man had done, Josiah could not justify so brutal a slaying. "You didn't have to kill him, Tyree," he said finally. "You could have taken him in."

The driver nodded. "I could have," he admitted, "but I chose not to." He stepped away from Josiah, heading for the horses that were tethered at the trees just beyond the clearing.

Josiah grabbed his arm and pulled him back. "You *chose* to kill him," he accused. What Tyree had done thoroughly repulsed him, almost as much as what Tyree had nearly allowed to happen.

Tyree peeled the man's fingers from his arm. He could stand it no longer. "You think that was murder," he said, having no trouble saying the word. "Lassiter deserved to die." He nodded at the body of Elizabeth Simpson. "A life for a life," he mocked.

Josiah shook his head. He felt a great numbness in his chest, still unsure of what he felt for his younger wife, but certain as to what he felt about Tyree's decision to kill a man he could have made his prisoner. "You don't have the right to make that judgment!" he declared righteously. He was thinking as much of himself as he was thinking of the dead man. "To bend the Scriptures to suit your needs . . ."

"And why not?" Tyree demanded. "I have as much right to judge who should die as *you* have to judge who should live! As for bending the Scriptures to suit *my* needs, isn't that what you did when you found yourself wanting to bed a girl damned near young enough to be your daughter?"

Josiah's face flushed a bright crimson. "That's a lie," he rasped.

"I don't think so," Tyree declared flatly. He poked a finger at the man's chest. "You hide behind your religion, Simpson, like some goddamned coward. You hide behind your God and blame everyone else for your failings!" He broke away from Josiah, once more heading for the horses that waited at the edge of the clearing.

Josiah shouted after him. "And you, Tyree! What do you hide behind?"

Tyree flinched, but kept on walking. "My job," he muttered.

It was true. He had spent a lot of years moving people and freight from one place to another, with little distinction between the two—all because he didn't care to get involved, to get hurt.

Like he was hurting right now. He had seen the look in Rebecca's eyes when he passed her. It was the same look he had observed in the long moments just before he shot and killed Kyle Lassiter, when he was still debating Josiah Simpson's fate.

He knew that Rebecca was afraid of him—of what he had almost done. He had allowed her to see a part of his nature that he had struggled for years to keep hidden, and she was afraid.

Tyree cursed and kept walking. He knew, now, just how much he loved her. Enough, he thought bitterly, to let Josiah Simpson remain alive.

Chapter Fifteen

Together, Billy Starbuck and Simon Tyree had succeeded in bringing the coach back to the cabin, where Josiah and Rebecca had assembled the sparse belongings they had salvaged from the wreckage. The four horses had been hitched up, and all the gold and paper currency had been stored under the driver's boot. Now Josiah and Rebecca stood on the porch with Tyree, who was watching Starbuck. The young man, who seemed more arrogant and brash than ever, was getting reacquainted with his recaptured black mare.

All that remained to be done was to bury the dead, and Rebecca sensed that Tyree had Starbuck in mind for the unpleasant task. She wanted to stop him, but he had surrendered to her once, when she had silently pleaded with him to help Josiah, and she knew he would not yield again. Still, she had to try. "Don't make him do this, Simon," she murmured. "Please."

He shook his head and gently removed her hand without looking at her. He crossed the yard and went to the place where Starbuck was working with the mare. "Come with me," he ordered softly, looking directly at the man. When the young outlaw didn't obey, he grabbed him by the scruff of the neck and shoved him toward the cabin, pausing there just long enough to pick up the shovel.

Tyree kept hold of Starbuck's neck, his fingers biting into the sensitive flesh between the ear and collarbone. When they reached the small clearing above the receding river, he stopped. None too gently, he spun the man around and pushed the short-handled spade into his exposed gut. "Start digging," he ordered.

Starbuck's eyes searched Tyree's for some small hint of compassion but found none. When he lowered his gaze and spied the blanket-shrouded bodies of Elizabeth Simpson and Kyle Lassiter, all bravado left his face. "I can't," he sobbed.

Tyree was unrelenting. "They're your dead," he said cruelly, placing the blame for both deaths squarely on the young man's shoulders. "You're going to bury them."

The outlaw's head snapped up. "That's not true!" he said vehemently. "Lassiter killed Beth, and you . . . *you* killed Lassiter!"

"That's right," Tyree said agreeably, nodding his head. "But you're the reason they were here. Just like you're the reason they're dead!"

Billy Starbuck was growing old, right before Tyree's eyes. The inner pain tearing at the young man robbed his face of its softness and drew tight lines around his nose and mouth. He stared at Elizabeth's shroud-covered body once more, fighting the tears. "I *loved* her," he said aloud.

"She was a whore," Tyree retorted angrily.

"Damn you!" he shot back. "*Goddamn you!*" He dropped the shovel and swung out with his fist.

Tyree blocked the blow easily. He backhanded the outlaw hard, right across the mouth, his hand arcing upward and back to slap him again, this time with his open palm. It was a measured blow intended to humiliate and produce tears, and it succeeded. "I told you to start digging," he declared harshly. "*Now!*"

Starbuck turned away, both hands wrapping around the handle of the shovel. He was crying. For some reason he did not understand, Tyree's slaps were harder to take than any of Josiah's clumsy attempts to discipline him had been. Fueled by his humiliation, the young man's anger peaked, his knuckles turning blue-white as he felt the urge to raise the shovel up above his own head and down again on Tyree's.

As if he had read Starbuck's mind, Tyree cuffed the younger man again, this time hard enough to knock him face down into the dirt. "Don't even think about it," he warned. He reached down and jerked the man upright. "Dig!" he ordered for the final time.

It was backbreaking work. Six inches down, the ground was still frozen, and the shovel was old and dull. Tyree was relentless in his supervision of the chore, pacing out the precise measurements of the two separate graves and voicing his loud disapproval each time Starbuck paused in his digging. Finally, both graves were finished, and together the two men lowered the bodies into the earth, Kyle Lassiter first and then the smaller, more petite body of Elizabeth Simpson.

Breathing hard, Starbuck stood beside the young woman's grave, his face ashen. Sweat mingled with his tears, and he wiped his sleeve across his eyes and nose. Regardless of what Elizabeth had said and done, he still cared for her, as a man always remembers his first love. "We should say *something*," he said in a quiet, intense whisper. "A prayer, some words . . ." His voice drifted off.

Coldly, Tyree kicked the first mound of dirt into the open grave. "She's beyond hearing any words you might have for her," he said, "and I don't believe in wasting prayers on the dead."

Hating Tyree more than he ever thought possible, Starbuck stared across at the man. "You bastard," he hissed.

Tyree shrugged and put the shovel back into the younger man's blistered hands. "Get it done," he instructed, clearly tolerating no disobedience.

Starbuck did as he was told. Slowly, the physical pain, the burning ache in his hands and back, began to dull the hurt that was in his heart. But not the anger. Finished, he threw the shovel down at Tyree's feet.

Tyree had been busy while Starbuck worked. He

picked up the tool and thrust it back into the younger man's chest. "One more," he said, pointing to a third plot he had outlined in the melting snow and wet sand.

Still not thinking clearly, Starbuck mindlessly began to dig again, and then, slowly, his senses returned. "Three?" he said, mystified. "Why three?" When he looked up, he was staring directly into the hollow blackness of the barrel of Tyree's revolver.

"Billy Starbuck," Tyree replied, smiling. "I'm going to bury Billy Starbuck!"

"Billy Starbuck?" the younger man echoed weakly.

Tyree nodded. "The reward. Ten thousand dollars, dead or alive." He let the words sink in. "I think *dead* is a hell of a lot easier than *alive*. You caused me a lot of grief, boy," he said evenly. "You damn near got me killed, and you made me feel and look like a damned fool. You used to *work* for me, boy. For the line. I trusted you."

The outlaw swallowed hard. Everything Tyree was saying was true. Desperately, he appealed to the man, hoping to strike at the one weakness he had perceived in the driver's tough veneer. "Rebecca," he said slyly. "You kill me, Rebecca will hate your guts." He smiled triumphantly, knowing from the brief flicker of pain in Tyree's eyes that he had guessed right. His feeling of elation was short-lived.

His expression and tone were cold and threatening as Tyree said, "Don't hide behind the woman, boy."

The young outlaw's temper flared again. Indignant, he tried to speak, the words failing to come. "I'm . . ." he sputtered, "I'm not . . . *not* hiding!"

"The hell you aren't," Tyree snapped disgustedly. "You're trying to hide behind her skirts, just like you've hid behind this." He lifted the corner of Billy Starbuck's neckerchief with the barrel of his gun. The cold metal was like the hand of death as it brushed across the young man's neck. Tyree smiled, mocking the boy. "You hid behind that mask the same way your brother hid behind his religion!"

The comparison with Josiah angered the outlaw as

much as the accusation that he was a coward—a coward who had to hide behind a mask, a false name, and a woman. "That's a lie!" he raged, knowing deep inside that it was the truth.

"Is it?" Tyree snorted. "You were a boy, playing a boy's game, until . . ." He nodded at the two graves and then at the partly dug one Starbuck was standing in. "Game's over," he announced with an air of finality. His eyes were filled with the same indifference that had turned them the color of gray slate earlier when he had faced Kyle Lassiter and had killed him. "Time to pay the piper." He cocked the gun and fired.

Billy Starbuck fell. In the distance Rebecca screamed.

Will Simpson came to slowly, aware of a terrible ringing in his left ear, the acrid scent of scorched hair pungent in the air about his head. And he was cold, deathly cold. A chorus of muted voices sounded around and above him.

Still unsure, Will opened his eyes. A sea of concerned faces hovered over him: Rebecca, Josiah, and Simon Tyree. "What happened?" he croaked weakly.

Rebecca pulled the blanket up around the young man's bare shoulders. "You fainted." Her brow knotted as she remembered the myriad of emotions that had swept through her when she heard the shot and ran to find her brother-in-law on the ground—her panic and her anger and the sudden feeling of gratitude that had followed as she understood Tyree's perverse charade in pretending to shoot Will.

Not feeling the need to explain, Tyree tossed the young man a change of clothes, which he had dug from beneath the ruined bed. "Get dressed," he ordered.

Will knew better than to disobey. He sat upright, his head hurting too much to prompt even a brief argument with the man. He dressed in complete silence, aware only of Rebecca's weak smile of reassurance.

Tyree was standing near the cabin when Will finished

dressing. He gestured for the young man to follow him and then led the way down into the yard.

Three graves stood before them. The stone-capped cairn nearest the cabin was marked by the elaborately decorated stock of Billy Starbuck's Winchester Centennial, the barrel of the rifle completely buried in the sand and rock. Tyree pointed to the grave, his hand closing around Will's wrist when the young man reached out in a futile attempt to retrieve the treasured weapon.

"Billy Starbuck," Tyree said, nodding at the grave. "His clothes, his mask, his boots. Everything that was Billy Starbuck," he finished. Everything, he reminded himself, except the small-caliber handgun Josiah Simpson had found in Will's cabin and which Josiah now carried in his right front pocket. Tyree answered the young man's next question without being asked. "I turned her loose," he said, nodding toward the thick scrub. The black mare was as much of a legend as Billy Starbuck himself.

Giving the younger man no chance to argue, Tyree turned away from him, his next words directed at Josiah. "How old is he?" he asked, talking as if Will were too dense to answer himself.

"Nineteen," Josiah answered, his eyes searching his brother's pale face. "He turned nineteen the fourteenth of March."

Tyree nodded. Will Simpson was just three years younger than his own son—the son he had lost. His hand was still wrapped around Will's wrist. "If I turn him in," he began, his voice harsh yet somehow soft, "he's going to go to prison. Fifteen, maybe twenty, years . . . if he doesn't hang," he finished grimly.

Josiah's jaw tightened. He was thinking about the embarrassment his younger brother had caused him—and would continue to cause him if he went to trial. "What do you want, Tyree?" he asked. "To let him go?" He thought then of the reward that had been offered for Billy Starbuck's capture, and of the words Tyree had spoken beside the open grave. He could only hope that the man would be willing to settle for a great deal less. "How much?" he finally asked.

Tyree grinned. "I want Will," he answered, "from now until he comes of age." He felt the young man try to pull away and held him fast. "Two years against twenty," he bargained, more for Will's benefit than for Josiah's.

"No!" Will exploded stubbornly. "*No!*"

Surprisingly, it was Rebecca that responded. "Be quiet, Will," she ordered. "Please, just be quiet." Her motives in hearing Tyree out were completely unselfish, although it would be some time before Will understood. It was more than the welfare of the baby now asleep inside the coach, the little boy Will stubbornly believed was his and who Rebecca loved as her own. She couldn't bear to think of her brother-in-law in prison—or worse, at the end of a rope. "And if we agree, Simon?" she asked quietly.

"I'll do my damndest to make a man of him," Tyree promised her. "An *honest* man."

Josiah Simpson exhaled loudly, visibly relieved that Tyree did not want money. The driver's proposal pleased him, and that pleasure showed plainly in his face. "You're going to go with Tyree, Will. You're going to stay with him." He reached out to touch his brother's arm and felt the young man pull away.

"You've got no right," Will argued. "No right at all!"

Tyree shook his head. "You're wrong, boy," he said firmly. "Like it or not, from now until the day you turn twenty-one, he's got every right in the world to say where you live, and with who. That *who* is going to be me," he informed the young man, smiling as though he took considerable pleasure in the telling.

"I'll run," Will declared belligerently.

Tyree smiled more broadly than before. "Just try," he suggested, sounding as if he wished the young man would attempt it.

There was only one alternative left for Will Simpson. He turned his eyes on his brother and then on Rebecca. "I'll come home," he offered hopefully, appealing more to the woman than to his brother. "It'll be different." He knew it was a lie, but that didn't stop him from saying the words.

Rebecca shook her head. She loved Will enough to let him go, to do what was best for him. She and Josiah would never be able to give Will what he needed.

"Shit!" the youth cursed. "Some choice—twenty years in the can, or two years with Simon Tyree as a jailer! Holy shit!"

Tyree pulled the young man close. "You ever been taught how to talk in front of a lady?"

"Yes!" Will shouted. "Of course I have. Yes," he repeated more contritely.

"Yes, *what*?" Tyree demanded.

Will heaved a great sigh. He felt Tyree's fingers dig into his upper arm. "Yes, sir," he whispered. He could not believe that he said the words—and that for some time to come he would be saying them again and again.

Josiah stared across the deceptively smooth river, his arms folded across his chest. "What now, Tyree?" he asked. The pretense between the two men still existed, neither one of them willing to say what was truly on his mind.

Tyree contemplated for a long moment, rubbing his chin. "We'll stay on this side," he said finally, indicating the place along the bank that had been cleared in the wake of the sudden spring flood. It would be rough going, sloughing through the wet sand, but they would make it.

Josiah cleared his throat. "Rebecca," he said softly, feeling awkward. He knew how close he was to losing his wife to Simon Tyree, and he had made up his mind not to let it happen. "My wife," he said, the animosity finally evident in his tone, "wants to speak with you, Mr. Tyree." There was something final in his announcement, and without another word he walked away.

Tyree watched as Josiah met Rebecca on the path leading to the cabin and paused just long enough to say something to her before reaching out to touch her arm. His hand lingered on her forearm as they parted, as if he were trying to hold her back, but she slipped from beneath his fingers and moved away. He watched her intently as she trudged through the wet sand toward Tyree.

"Simon," she began, her voice soft and hesitant. She was holding Benjamin, wide awake now in her arms.

Tyree chose not to look at her, his eyes first sweeping the little boy and then settling on the young man in the driver's box. "Will's going to be all right," he said finally.

"I know that, Simon," she replied. She was quiet for a time. "I owe you so much," she said. She buried her head against the softness of Benjamin's blond curls, and unable to stop herself, she began to cry.

Tyree took them both in his arms. He held them for a moment and then, tenderly, pushed both of them away to a safer distance, one hand on each arm as he spoke. "I love you, Rebecca," he said softly. "And I hurt too damned much to let you go without saying the words. I've been sorry for a lot of things in my life, but I'm not sorry for telling you what I feel. Come with me."

He paused, collecting her against his chest. And then he kissed her, a long, passionate kiss that said much more than his words.

She yielded and then pulled away, a wave of diverse emotions sweeping through her, leaving her at once elated and drained. It had been a long time since a man—any man—had kissed her with such passion.

And still she was torn. She half turned, staring back at her husband. Out of the corner of her eye, she saw Simon, and beyond him Will, pensive and perched high in the driver's box of the great Concord. The young man's eyes spoke eloquently: *Come with us, Rebecca.*

Resolutely, the woman composed herself and then turned back to face Tyree. When he tried to take her in his arms again, she held out her hand, stopping him. "He's my husband, Simon." She was doing a bad job of trying to explain what she was feeling, but she could not stop the words. "No matter what he's done or what he hasn't done, a part of me still loves him. Almost as much as I've learned to love you," she said, wishing that things could be different. "I made a promise the day I married Josiah." She raised her hand, pressing her fingers against Tyree's lips when he attempted to speak, shaking her head at the thoughts that were so evident in his eyes. "To God. *My* God," she finished quietly.

Tyree's jaws tightened, and he nodded his head. It was not that he could understand what she felt or why she would remain faithful to a man who had been so blind to her worth. But, he thought, considering, it was partly Rebecca's fidelity, her stubborn faithfulness to her husband, that had made him love her. "If you ever change your mind, I'll always be ready for you," he said softly, knowing in his heart that she never would.

She smiled up at him, touching his face with her hand. "You're a good man, Simon Tyree," she murmured, biting her lips to stop their trembling. "In another time, another place . . ." She could not finish; there was no point in speculating about what could have been. Yielding to her own needs a final time, she tenderly kissed Tyree's cheek.

Josiah Simpson stood apart from the others, keenly aware of the quiet words between Simon Tyree and his wife, wishing desperately that he could hear what was being said. Without thinking, his hand groped for the pistol deep in his right front pocket, his fingers closing around the small pearl-handled grip.

It was all so unfair, he grieved. He had been a good husband, a good provider. Rebecca had never known hunger or any of the other deprivations so common among other frontier wives.

She *belonged* to him. With God as their witness, she had pledged herself to him, had sworn her love for him. Just as he had sworn his love to her.

Enjoying his martyrdom, Josiah continued to reflect on his miseries. None of it was his fault, he reasoned. The war had changed him, but for the better: all the brutality, the slaughter, had drawn him closer to God, and to the Solomonites. Afterward, he had assumed his role as head of the family, caring for his widowed mother when his father died and raising his own brother.

Josiah's gaze shifted to the place where Will Simpson sat atop the big Concord. Much of what had happened between him and Rebecca was Will's fault, he thought, recalling the many times they had quarreled over his brother. He marked that as the real beginning of their troubles.

One by one, Josiah examined the problems and tragedies of his life. And each time, he found himself faultless. In the end, the blame for everything that happened—*everything*—lay at the feet of another. The major who had been his commanding officer during the long brutal sweep toward the sea, the young brother who had turned outlaw, the faithless young wife who had borne a bastard child . . .

Simon Tyree, the itinerant and Godless stage driver who was trying to steal his wife.

The pistol was cold against Josiah's fingers. He took it out of his pocket, absently exposing the cylinder and counting the cartridges. He was remembering the look on Tyree's face in those tense moments before Kyle Lassiter died, and that memory justified what he was about to do.

And then he saw Rebecca kiss Tyree.

Josiah's chest rose and fell, the skin feeling tight across his heart. The picture before him—the vision of Rebecca, Benjamin, and Tyree—burned into his very soul.

Benjamin. The one failure Josiah could not deny. He could never love the child. Never. And he could never sire another.

Josiah raised the pistol. He aimed directly at Simon Tyree's broad forehead. And then the barrel of the pistol, the small copper-bead sight, drifted slowly to the left and down, centering on the topmost curl on Benjamin's small head.

Desperation clawed at the man's belly. He realized that he could not bear the thought of losing Rebecca any more than he could bear the thought of raising Elizabeth's bastard son. And yet, if he denied the baby, if he did anything to hurt him . . . Tyree would win, he thought bitterly.

It was losing the game that troubled Josiah—the scandal and the terrible whispers that would haunt him for the rest of his life. He would be ridiculed, reviled by his peers if he and Rebecca parted.

And if there was a divorce, if she gave herself to another man . . .

A flicker of hope filled Josiah Simpson's small and troubled heart. Rebecca would never leave him if he were hurt, would never turn her back on him if he truly needed her.

He would win, he reasoned. He would keep what was rightfully his, and as for Benjamin . . . He could not love the boy, he knew, but he could learn to *pretend* to love him.

Josiah turned the pistol on himself. It would have been better, he thought, if he could have arranged a confrontation with Tyree, a situation where the driver would be at fault, but that was risky, far too risky. He had no doubt that, given a second chance, Tyree would kill him. *No*, he thought, *it's better this way. Rebecca will think I tried to kill myself because I loved her and couldn't bear to lose her. And her guilt will bind her to me.*

He pressed the barrel to his side, shrewdly calculating the kind of wound that would maim but not kill him. *Time. I need to buy myself and Rebecca a little time— without Will, without Simon Tyree.*

He pulled the trigger. There was surprisingly little pain at first, and then an incredible burning as the bullet impacted against his lower rib. The soft piece of lead shattered and separated, one piece lodging in the soft muscles in his lower back, the other plunging downward and exiting at his groin.

Josiah fell to his knees, his eyes widening in terror as a great spurt of bright red blood poured from the hole in the side of his trousers. The flow increased and decreased in time to the beat of his heart, and the feeble pressure of his hand against the wound did nothing to stem the flow.

*   *   *

Rebecca and Tyree heard the muted crack of the pistol, neither one of them understanding what was happening. And then they saw.

The driver took Benjamin in his arms, calling out to Will as he followed Rebecca back up the path toward the cabin. They were running, both of them, Will only scant yards behind them.

All three of them arrived at Josiah's side at the same time. Rebecca fell to her knees beside her husband, her hands busily exploring the terrible wound in his side. The stench of urine mingled with the salty aroma of warm blood, and she knew at once that he was dying. "Josiah," she whispered. The helplessness she felt was unbearable.

Tyree said nothing. He sat the puzzled baby down in the sand at his side, his own exploration of Josiah's injury less gentle than the woman's. "You fool," he breathed, the earlier pretense gone. "You goddamned fool!"

Josiah pushed Tyree's hand away, still possessed with the need to win. He groped for Rebecca's hand, his fingers lacing hers and holding her tight. "For you," he rasped gallantly. If he was going to die, it was going to be a noble death. "So you would be free."

She collapsed back on her heels. "I was going to stay with you, Josiah," she murmured. "*I was going to stay with you!*"

Josiah's eyes were lit with a peculiar fire, and he turned them on Tyree before gazing again at his wife. "His fault," he said. "He was going to take you away. . . ."

Will Simpson laughed. It was a cruel sound, sardonic and harsh against the sudden quiet. Embarrassed, the young man faced his sister-in-law, seeing the guilt beginning to draw lines against her pale cheeks. "He did it for himself, Rebecca," he said finally. As if to make his point, he picked up the small pistol Josiah had dropped in the sand. The barrel was so small, the opening barely as large as the little finger of Benjamin's tiny hand. When he saw that the woman did not understand his meaning, he stood up, pulling Benjamin with him and hugging him tight.

"I'm glad!" he yelled. "Do you hear me, Josiah? I'm glad you messed it up!" Fighting his tears, he backed away.

Josiah Simpson could feel his life draining away. He lay still, his head resting in Rebecca's lap, the sun above him distant and cold. *It wasn't supposed to be like this,* he thought. He tried to rise up and could not; he called out for his wife. "Forever," he croaked, still trying desperately to bind her to him, his voice failing him. "You belong to me forever." And then the growing darkness swallowed him, and he died.

Tyree reached out, his hand gentle and warm against Rebecca's shoulder, angry when she tried to pull away. "It was his choice, Rebecca," he said firmly. "His way out." He knew what Will had been trying to say: that Josiah had never intended to kill himself. *Damn you,* he silently cursed, staring at the man's body. *Damn you!*

She nodded her head, not really believing him. As hard as she fought to deny the feeling, it was still there: that somehow she could have stopped what had happened, could have kept Josiah from destroying himself. She could feel herself being consumed by guilt. "I need to be alone, Simon," she said finally.

Tyree stood staring at Rebecca, watching as she bade her final farewell to Josiah. She stood, quiet and vulnerable, beside her husband's grave, her lips silently moving. And then she turned away.

Her stride changed as she moved down the pathway, her back straightening and her head lifting as she seemed to restore herself. The old strength was returning, the courage Tyree had seen and admired in the very beginning, and he was filled with a sense of awe and unabashed pride as he watched her approach.

She was still able to smile, and he saw that some of the pain was already gone from her incredible green eyes. He returned the smile, saying nothing, holding Benjamin out to her and not pulling back when their fingers touched. He tried to speak. "Benjamin," he began. He felt the fool when the other words failed to come.

Rebecca smoothed the baby's curls and then pulled him tight against her chest. "I'm going to be all right, Simon," she said resolutely. She was genuinely sad that things had ended as they had, but not regretful, and no longer guilty. "You were right." She turned, able to face the grave and see it in its proper perspective. "It *was* Josiah's choice."

He found his voice. "And now?" he asked gently. He started to touch her cheek, changing his mind and letting his hand caress Benjamin's small face instead. The baby giggled and grabbed at his thumb.

Rebecca studied Tyree's face, searching his very soul with her eyes. So much had transpired in the past few days—so much had passed between them. "Time," she said finally. "I need some time, Simon."

Tyree's chest lifted and then fell as he inhaled deeply. There was a chance, he rejoiced silently. After everything that had happened, he really had a chance!

He helped her into the coach, taking longer than he should as he arranged the baby on the seat next to her. "We'll go to Flagstaff," he announced. "and you'll have a warm bed, a hot meal . . ." He chucked the baby's chin with his thumb and forefinger. "And a bath."

Rebecca laughed, sharing Tyree's memory of the time at the way station—the way he had bathed Benjamin and tended to his needs.

Their eyes met, but they said nothing; there was no need to say anything. Tyree nodded and backed out of the coach, feeling better than he had in a long, long time.

He stepped down onto the ground, slamming the door shut and digging into his pockets for his gloves. "You about done fooling around with my horses, boy?" he boomed, shouting up at the young man who was in his seat.

"I got a name, Simon," Will answered. "It's Billy. Billy Star . . . Will Simpson," he finished, extending his hand.

Tyree shook his head as he climbed up into the driver's box and took the reins. "Will Simpson," he repeated and shook his head again. He thought on it awhile and then cast a sidewise look at the young man. He was going to make this legal, he decided. As soon as they reached Flagstaff and were settled in, he was going to find a lawyer, a good lawyer who would affect a quick and legal adoption. If he was also going to have all the grief, all the responsibilities, he was also going to have some of the joys. "Tyree," he said finally. "Will Tyree."

The young man considered Tyree's words, so deep in thought that he didn't feel the slight leeward sway of the coach as the driver urged the horses into an awkward trot. "Will Simpson Tyree," he declared finally, writing the words out before him in the empty air, never once looking back as the ruins of his old hideaway disappeared behind them. He brightened and began to laugh. It was as if he could actually see the name inscribed on paper. Or on the side of a stagecoach, his own stagecoach, he thought.

"I'll drive, old man," he announced, reaching for the reins. In his mind's eye, he could already see himself as the greatest stage driver in the territory.

"Not hardly." Tyree laughed, refusing to let go of the ribbons. "You've got a lot to learn before I turn you loose with one of my wagons!"

The younger man was unperturbed. The vision of his new name loomed before him again, in print this time, on the cover of Ned Buntline's magazine and Beadle's dime novels . . . and *Harpers Weekly*! "I'm going to write," he announced suddenly. "For Buntline and Harpers!" The sudden change in professions—from outlaw, to stage driver, to writer—didn't bother him. He had time, lots of time. And when he was old, really old, like Tyree, he would write a book.

"Billy Starbuck," he said aloud, ducking when Tyree took a swing at his head. "I'll write all about the true adventures of Billy Starbuck and how he stole from the rich to give to the poor!"

Tyree closed his eyes, wishing that he could close his ears. Will raved on, his conversation growing more animated with each passing quarter mile as he recounted the adventures, mostly imagined, of the fearless outlaw Billy Starbuck. Like all the young, he was healing fast.

Too fast, Tyree reckoned, muttering a quick prayer for strength for himself, while begging for a sudden case of laryngitis for his young ward. "Please, God," he whispered.

God wasn't listening. If anything, Will's voice grew stronger. Tyree breathed yet another prayer, using the whip to push the horses at an even faster clip. The mud and water splashed high up on the sides of the coach as the Concord skimmed surprisingly well across the wet terrain. Will's voice and words carried above the noise and grew louder.

Simon Tyree gritted his teeth. It was going to be a long haul between Devil's Canyon and the end of the line.